Who's the Boss?

"It needs work," Simon says again. . . . "For one thing, the stage directions are sketchy — "

"I thought that was your job," I say.

"It looks like it'll have to be. Listen, I'll just do the necessary changes for you, okay? That'll save us a lot of time and aggravation."

"No." Simon looks at me and I shake my head. " . . . no, it's not okay with me for you to make the changes. Your job is directing, not writing."

"I was just trying to save you some work. I thought that was what you'd want."

It might have been what I wanted a few hours ago, but now I knew I'd scratch his eyes out before I'd let him touch one word of my play.

D0868000

Other Point paperbacks
you will want to read:

Herb Seasoning
by Julian F. Thompson

Paradise Lane
by William Taylor

Sheila's Dying
by Alden Carter

Life Without Friends
by Ellen Emerson White

Acts of Love
by Maureen Daly

point

Something's Rotten in the State of Maryland

Laura A. Sonnenmark

SCHOLASTIC INC.
New York Toronto London Auckland Sydney

ISBN 0-590-42877-2

12 11 10 9 8 7 6 5 4 3 2 1   11   1 2 3 4 5 6/9

To Les, because he believed.

To Mom, because I miss her.

Something's Rotten in the State of Maryland

One

Ask anyone who knows me, and they'll tell you that Marie Valpacchio is a very easygoing person. The truth is, I'm lazy. Arguing with people is just too much trouble. Besides, I've spent most of my life listening to my parents battle it out with each other. Believe me, after living in a war zone for that long, you crave peace. At any price.

Over the years I've learned an easier way to get along with people. You smile, you agree, and then you do or think whatever it is you want to do or think, only in private. That's my surefire method of survival in these troubled times, and in nearly seventeen years it hasn't failed me yet.

It was my friend Tina who pointed out the fact that I'm lazy, and after giving it careful consideration, I have to admit she's right. Only I don't think of it as being lazy, more like being *satisfied*. Which you have to admit sounds a lot better.

Take my grades, for example. I do pretty well, but I'm definitely not the overachiever type. Making the honor roll is *not* my life's ambition. I'm quite willing to coast along with my B average so I can accommodate my social life.

Then there's my appearance. I'm on the short side, with dark hair and eyes, and very fair skin. When I was little my mother always dressed me up for Halloween as Snow White. As much as I hated it, it is true that I made a very good Snow White. I still would. Who knows? Maybe one day I'll get a job at Disney World.

Looking like an angelic cartoon character hasn't hurt me any. Furthermore, although I'm honestly not conceited, I know I could be great-looking if I really put some effort into it. But I figure, why bother? I already have a boyfriend who thinks I'm cute. Even if that's not as good as beautiful, it's good enough for me. I've never been the type of person who needs a lot of attention from the opposite sex anyway.

As for being popular, frankly, that's *way* too much work. I'm *satisfied*, you see, with things just the way they are.

It was due to my basic laziness that I ended up in a class called Shakespeare's Tragic Heroes. I'd neglected to fill out my class registration card on time, and this class was the only one that I either hadn't taken before or that wasn't already full. I consoled myself with the fact that since Mr. Phillips was also the drama teacher, the class couldn't be *that* hard. I figured we'd probably

2

sit around and talk about character motivation and easy stuff like that.

Boy, was I wrong. Mr. Phillips dresses casually — jeans and long hair that show he's a holdout from the sixties — but his attitude toward old Will is very, very serious. And heaven help you if yours is not equally so. We not only had to read three very heavy and boring plays, we also had to be prepared to discuss them in detail. With a title like Shakespeare's Tragic Heroes, you don't expect a lot of laughs, and believe me, there haven't been any.

First there was Othello, who is this crazy person who strangles his doormat of a wife in a fit of jealousy. Then there was Macbeth, who goes mad with ambition and kills all his houseguests. (Like the Roach Motel: You can check in, but you can't check out.) Of course, having a wife like Lady Macbeth would send anyone over the edge.

And then there was my personal favorite, Hamlet, the melancholy prince of Denmark, who either kills, or is responsible for the killing of, practically the whole cast. Which left me to wonder who was going to rule Denmark now that the entire royal family was wiped out, but Mr. Phillips said that was irrelevant.

And people complain about the violence on television! The writers of *Nightmare on Elm Street* have nothing on Shakespeare, who certainly knew his blood and gore.

I'm thinking all about this one perfectly ordinary Tuesday, when I notice Mr. Phillips is handing back term papers — the ones that are worth forty percent of our grade. I also notice that everyone has gotten one back but me.

"Please see me after class, Marie," he tells me, and my heart takes a dive into the pit of my stomach. Out of the corner of my eye I see the other kids exchange looks. We all know why he wants to see me, and why he didn't hand back my paper in front of everyone. He doesn't want them to see the big fat F scrawled across the top of it.

Nice guy.

My heart repositions itself and starts beating again, but I'm feeling slightly sick. I don't want to stay after class. I don't want to see that F and hear Mr. Phillips talk about how disappointed he is in me, how he expected better from a student who once represented her fifth-grade class in the Magothy Beach Elementary School spelling bee.

On the other hand, maybe he isn't disappointed. Maybe F work is what he expects from the girl who misspelled *exhilarating*, and he wants me to stay after to tell me so.

The funny thing is, I didn't think I'd done such a bad job of it. The assignment, I mean. Mr. Phillips had given us a choice: rewrite the last act of one of the plays, write a completely new act, or write a term paper tying all three plays together. We could even write a whole play, he had said with a grin. Fat chance of anyone crazy enough to do that.

Only I am. Crazy enough, that is.

I'd procrastinated so long that I really didn't have much choice. I didn't have the time to do the research for a term paper. I find those things pretty boring, anyway. I can never find anything to say that hasn't been said before, so what's the point? Rewriting an act from one of the plays was out of the question, since

4

I can't even write one *sentence* in the kind of English they had in Shakespeare's day.

Then I thought about *West Side Story*, which is basically *Romeo and Juliet*, only set in this century and in New York City. Mr. Phillips says there are lots of examples of old plays being redone, so I thought, Why not a modern *Hamlet*? How hard could it be? The story was already there; all I had to do was modernize it a bit and write the dialogue.

So I sat down in front of our computer and began. And you know, once I got into it, it was sort of fun. Which by itself should have told me something. Having fun and getting a good grade don't usually go hand in hand.

I'm not really paying attention to what is going on in class. The bell rings. Everyone jumps up to leave, filing past me with sympathetic and curious looks. Mandy Shelton whispers that I can call her later for the notes I didn't take. And then we're alone.

Mr. Phillips frowns at me from over his papers. "Do you know why I wanted to see you, Marie?" he asks. I give him my very best wide-eyed, innocent look.

"Something about my play?"

"Precisely." He looks at me in this very serious way he has. "It is *yours*, isn't it? You wrote it by yourself?"

"Yes."

"You didn't get any help? Your parents, perhaps an older brother or sister?"

"No. No way."

"Well!" He sits back and shakes his head. "Well!" he repeats, "all I can say is that I'm astounded. Simply astounded. That *you* . . . I would have never thought that *you* of all my students. . . ." He shakes his head

5

again. "It's a fine play, Marie. Such depth! Such insight! It's unbelievable!"

"Gee . . . thanks." Somehow my mind receives the message that he's complimenting me, and I smile. Then I think about the way he said *"you,"* and that he didn't even believe at first that I had written it, and I'm not so sure I should be smiling.

"Does that mean I get an A, Mr. Phillips?"

He beams at me. "Marie, I'm not only giving you an A, I'm giving *your* play to the Thespian Society for them to produce this February. Think of it, a real student production, directed, acted, and most importantly, *written* by students of Magothy High! It'll be a first for this school — maybe the entire state. We'll make history!"

"Wow," I mutter weakly. I've never thought of myself as the history-making type.

"And you'll be in on every decision, right from the start," he continues with mounting enthusiasm. "There's a lot to be done, of course, but you'll be working side by side with the director. We won't forget that this is *your* baby."

At the mention of work, my inner radar starts emitting warning signals. I picture myself painting scenery and moving set designs. Actual physical *labor* — not on your life!

"Gee, I'm really glad you like it, but I don't know if I'll be able to help out much. It sounds like a big time commitment, and I'm kind of booked up right now as it is with extracurricular activities. . . ." I smile and say a little prayer that he doesn't ask me to name all these extracurricular activities. Rushing home to watch *Santa Barbara* is about the only thing I do in the afternoon.

Mr. Phillips looks stunned for a moment, then gives me this real pitying smile, like I'm some kind of lunatic. You poor, ignorant girl, he's thinking, you don't have the sense to realize the honor you've been given. "Well, come to our meeting on Thursday after school. You'll want to meet the other kids at least, and I know they'll want to discuss your play with you." He pats my shoulder. "Between us, I'm sure we can work something out."

There's that word again. Ugh! I collect my books and head for the cafeteria.

Brian — my boyfriend — is already there in his usual seat, with a group of his jock buddies and their girlfriends. He's gotten my lunch for me, and even if it is meatloaf, which I detest, I thank him. It's not every guy who would be so thoughtful.

"Hey, I heard you got called after class to see Phillips," he says as I take my seat next to him. "What did he want with you?"

News travels fast in my school. "Remember the assignment I was working on about two weeks ago — you know, when I couldn't go bowling with you?"

"Ah, sure, a term paper, right?"

"Well, actually it was a play. Mr. Phillips kept me after to tell me how much he liked it and that they want to produce it."

"Who's they?"

"The drama cl — I mean, the Thespian Society."

The other kids around the table jump in.

"You wrote a *play*?"

"A *whole* play?"

"What's it about?"

"I didn't know you were the intellectual type!"

"Yeah," Brian says, looking at me strangely. "I didn't even know you could write."

"I didn't know, either," I tell him.

"How come you don't write for the school paper?"

"No one reads the school paper." Which is true. "Besides, I'm not interested in that kind of writing."

"I didn't know you were interested in any kind of writing," he says, and again there's a note in his voice that lets me know he isn't too sure he likes this new development. "You won't have to spend a lot of time on this — you know, like going to rehearsals, will you?"

"I'm not sure I'll be attending any rehearsals." Brian looks relieved, and I *know* what he's thinking. Football season is over, and baseball practice won't start for another few months. In the meantime he's got time to spare and he's planning to spend it with me.

"But if I do," I add, just to cover all my bases, "I think the rehearsals only last about six weeks."

"That's not so bad." I think this is an understatement, considering how long the football and baseball seasons last — and Brian likes me to go to all the games and cheer him on.

"Well, that's great, Marie," he says, putting an arm around me and giving me a little hug. "I'm proud of you. Real proud."

Everyone around the table begins pumping me for more information, but I can see Brian hasn't yet adjusted to the idea of having a girlfriend who's also a budding playwright — heck, I haven't adjusted to it yet myself. So I maneuver the conversation around to the upcoming Christmas vacation, and that makes both of us more comfortable.

For once when my parents ask me what happened at school that day I've got something to tell them. They look surprised but also very pleased.

"It doesn't really surprise me," Mom says, which I know is a lie. "I remember how you used to write little poems in elementary school."

"Mom, I did not. I hate poetry."

"You also wrote stories — they were quite good. It must be a wonderful play for them to want to put it on. When do rehearsals start?"

I shift a little in my seat and tell her I'm not sure I want to take an active part in the production.

"Of course you do," Dad says. "The playwright always works closely with the director and cast. And it is *your* play. You want them to do it right, don't you?"

At the other end of the table Mom is nodding vigorously. Just my luck. For once she and Dad are agreeing on something. "This is one opportunity you can't pass up," she says. "It's about time you developed some interests."

"I have interests!"

Mom doesn't bother to answer that. She just gives me a look that reminds me that mothers aren't as easy to fool as English teachers. She knows the truth about me and the afternoon soaps.

"The thing is," I say, squirming again, "it'll probably take up a lot of time."

"It seems to me that time is the one thing you have plenty of."

9

"This will look very good on your college applications," Dad adds meaningfully, and that's about the end of the discussion as far as my parents are concerned. They look so happy, so compatible, that I feel guilty even thinking about not going to that drama — *Thespian* Society meeting.

After dinner I call Tina. You could say Tina is my best friend, only we don't hang out together much anymore. Since getting to high school we've kind of drifted. We didn't have a fight or anything like that; it's just that our lives have taken different turns. She plays the oboe in the band, so she spends most of her time with that crowd. And since I've been dating Brian, I mostly spend time with the other jocks' girlfriends. But I still talk to Tina about the important things, because I know she'll always be there for me.

She's very excited about my news, but is nice enough not to act too surprised. Maybe she isn't surprised. I let her read some of it before I handed it in, and she'd told me then she thought it was good.

"Now you'll get the chance to be with people who share your interests," she says. Tina is very big on having interests, just like my mother.

Right away I start thinking about the type of kids in the drama — *excuse* me, the *Thespian* Society. They're mostly artsy types, kind of pretentious, if you know what I mean. But they probably think that girls like me are all dumb and superficial, so I guess we're even.

"I don't have any interest in drama," I argue, but she laughs.

"Of course you do. You're a playwright, aren't you?"

"Oh, right," I say slowly. "I guess I am."

* * *

The drama club meeting is Thursday after school in the auditorium. I've stopped trying to remember to call them the Thespian Society since I decided the name is too pretentious to take seriously. This is America, for heaven's sake. Let them speak English like the rest of us.

They're all gathered around Mr. Phillips when I walk in, and judging by the way a hush falls over them the minute they see me, I know they've been talking about me. Hostile eyes seem to bore holes in me as I make my way down the aisle. *You are a stranger, the enemy. Get out.*

Naturally, I'm not feeling very comfortable.

"Young people don't like Shakespeare," Mr. Phillips is telling them, "because they don't see how he relates to them. They think his plays are boring because they don't take the time to understand them. That's why I'm so excited about this" — he waves a copy of my play at them — "Marie has successfully taken *Hamlet* right into the nineties!"

At this point he turns and beckons me over to his side. I stand there with a sickly grin plastered on my face, while he continues trying to sell them my play. They aren't buying any of it.

"I'm sure all of you have questions for our playwright," Mr. Phillips says after four or five minutes of continuous sales pitch. I freeze.

The faces that stare at me are frozen, too. Frozen in silence. It's so quiet in the auditorium you could hear the proverbial pin drop. Suddenly a boy on my far left coughs, and we all turn to him expectantly. He waves his hand to let us know this is a real cough, not a question. I sigh with relief.

11

"No one has any questions?" Mr. Phillips asks. "Sure?"

They're sure, they're sure, I think.

"Very well. Then let's introduce ourselves, shall we?"

Let's not and say we did.

He goes around the room, naming everyone. Some I know by sight, and some I don't. There's Sabrina Solowick, of course, Magothy High's leading lady. She's famous for her long red hair and weird, sophisticated clothes. Apparently she's deluded herself into believing that she lives in Manhattan instead of a small, boring suburb twenty miles south of Baltimore. Sabrina nods at me and tosses back her glorious flaming tresses. I can't help but stare. No exaggeration, she has the kind of hair I've — up until now — only read about in historical romances. You know, the ones with the sultry covers showing a couple in a passionate embrace and the heroine falling out of her clothes.

I also recognize Simon Conreith from one of my English classes last year. There's no way I could forget him; he dominated every class discussion. I swear he knew more about twentieth-century American novelists than the teacher did.

He's a very intense type, and today he's dressed — this is the absolute truth — entirely in black. Black boots, black jeans, black sweater. Even his hair is black. Right away I figure he and Sabrina must be an item, each of them being so dramatic looking. He looks me over quickly, raises one thick, black eyebrow as if to say, "Big deal," and turns away.

The rest of the group turns out to be pretty friendly. I start to relax. This isn't going to be so bad, after all.

And then I find out that Simon is the director, and I realize it's not going to be bad, it's going to be worse.

As soon as Mr. Phillips dismisses the group Simon saunters over to me. I give him my warmest smile. I'd have more luck smiling at a rock. Rocks have better personalities.

"It looks like we'll have to get together over Christmas vacation," he says, as if that were a fate akin to having his insides ripped out by aliens. "We'll need to discuss changes."

"Changes? But you haven't read it yet, have you?"

Again with the raising of the eyebrow. I suppose he thinks it makes him look like James Bond. I think it makes him look like a pompous jerk.

"I don't have to read it to know there'll be changes. We'll have to get rid of the title, first thing."

"What's wrong with the title? I thought it was kind of cute."

"It's cute, all right. And stupid. *Something is Rotten in the State of Maryland* sounds like the title of a comedy or a skit from *Saturday Night Live.*" He stops suddenly. "It is supposed to be a tragedy, right?"

"Yes! It's *very* tragic. There's enough death and destruction to satisfy the meanest person in the world."

"That's something, I guess." He sighs and looks at me again. "So what did you have to do to convince Phillips to take your play?"

The meanest person in the world is Simon Conreith. Absolutely. For a moment I stare, flabbergasted. In my whole life *no one* has ever spoken to me like this, especially not a boy, and especially not since the seventh grade, when I began to get curves.

"Hey, wait a minute," I protest. "This was *his* idea,

not mine. If you'd rather direct something else, why don't you just tell him so?"

"Because Phillips is committed to an all-student production. More like an all-student fiasco." Another sigh. I tell you, this guy is wasted as a director. He should be with the actors, hamming it up. "Never mind," he says. "It'll just have to wait until after Christmas. I'm tied up until then. Give me your phone number and I'll call you."

"Ah — couldn't this wait until after vacation?"

"You heard what Mr. Phillips said — tryouts are the week after we get back. We'll have to start fixing the thing before then if we want a play for the actors to read. So what's your number?"

I don't like the way he's talking about my play. I like even less the fact that I have to give him my number right in front of a dozen or so witnesses. Right away I begin to invent excuses in my mind for when he calls. Like maybe I could tell him we have out-of-town visitors. Or maybe I could get the flu. "So sorry," I'll say, "getting together to butcher my awful play with the stupid title will just have to be postponed."

On the other hand, maybe I could die. With Simon as determined as he is, death would probably be the only acceptable excuse.

Simon calls me the day after Christmas. It's just my bad luck that I answer the phone. I only answer because I'm expecting Brian to call.

"Let's meet at my house tomorrow," he says without even asking me how my Christmas was. "Is two o'clock good for you?"

"Er — wouldn't it be better to meet at the library?"

14

"Uh-uh. No privacy there. Here we can have the whole house to ourselves."

Ker-plunk, goes my heart. Really, I'm not some hysterical girl who thinks every guy is madly in love with her, but why is privacy so important? And why did he have to make "to ourselves" sound so *sinister*?

"I don't know. My boyfriend might have plans — "

"It'll only take a few hours. Can't he spare you?"

"Yes, but I don't think — "

"Don't think. Got a pen handy? I'll give you directions to my house."

Like I said, I hate to argue. I find a pencil and write down his address, wondering if I should tell Brian about this.

I don't have much choice, because as soon as I hang up with Simon, Brian calls and asks me to go skating with him the next day.

"I can't," I tell him, fingering the silver filigree necklace he gave me yesterday. It really is beautiful. I nearly started to cry when I opened the box because it was the same necklace I had admired at the mall about two months ago. I was really touched that Brian remembered a tiny incident like that.

"I've got to go over the play with the director," I explain. "How about tomorrow night?"

"No go. I need my sleep. We leave Thursday morning at the crack of dawn, remember?"

"Oh, right." Brian goes skiing with his family every year. "Then I'll come over to your house later, okay? Just for a little while. I'll even help you pack, if you want."

"Sure, come over, but there's not much to pack. We're only going for three days. I'll be home for New

15

Year's Eve. Hey, where are you meeting this guy?"

"At his house," I reply quickly, lightly. "I guess he's afraid to be seen in public with me. He probably has so many mean things to say that he thinks I'll start bawling and embarrass him."

There is silence on the other end of the phone while I hold my breath. "Is he putting the moves on you?"

"No! Of course not!" Forget that I'd been thinking the same thing a moment ago. Hearing Brian put it into words makes my fears seem totally ridiculous. I mean, Simon Conreith? Put the moves on me? The guy can't stand me. And the feeling is mutual!

"Yeah, well, if he tries anything. . . ."

"Brian, get serious," I say, thinking that the time between football and baseball is way too long. Brian is the kind of guy who needs a constant physical outlet. "He knows about you. He might be a creep, but he's not stupid. Besides, Simon Conreith thinks too much of himself to bother with someone like me. I told you, he talks to me like I'm some sort of sub-species he found under a microscope."

There is another silence while I hold my breath. "Yeah," he agrees finally. "He probably only likes smart girls."

So what does that make me, I wonder?

TWO

"Don't be so paranoid," Tina is telling me an hour later. We're at her house. "Brian didn't mean that you're stupid. He was probably too worried about you meeting Simon at his house to pay attention to what he was saying."

"Maybe. But meeting Simon is not such a big deal."

"Maybe it is to Brian. Do you think he's attracted to you?"

"Huh?"

"Simon, you dope."

"No way!" I exclaim. I can tell that Tina is waiting for more explanation. "No way!" I repeat, shaking my head.

"Oh, well," she says. "He is cute." She catches my look. "Not like Brian, though."

"This is true," I agree rather smugly. Brian is gor-

17

geous. Tall, blond, baby-blue eyes, a body that you could put on a calendar. The works. He's also very nice. The perfect boyfriend.

"So, how was your Christmas?" I ask, changing the subject.

"The usual. Mom pulled out all the stops. Turkey *and* ham, about a thousand different vegetables, and four different kinds of pie. God, I can't stand it. I think I gained about ten pounds."

"We went to Dad's side this year," I tell her. "In Baltimore. The usual arguments."

Perhaps I should explain the differences between Tina's family and mine. Tina's family is more like a family you would see on television. Tune in to the Beaver, and you get the general idea. Her mom is a whiz in the kitchen. The house is spotless, decorated with all kinds of homemade stuff right out of *Family Circle*. Her whole family gets along nicely and never argues.

My family, now that's another story. My father is a negotiator for a union, and my mother is a corporate lawyer. All they ever do is argue. Not just about the things most married people argue about, like money or where to go on vacation. They also argue about the minimum wage and U.S. policy in the Middle East. My twin brothers are just as bad. They're both in college. Paul is a business major, and Jack wants to save the world from nuclear disaster. Dinner with the four of them is like trying to eat during the battle of Gettysburg. Very bad for the digestion.

It's ten times worse when we all get together with either set of relatives, all of whom have tempers that fit any stereotypes you may have formed about the Irish

18

and the Italians. Those occasions are comparable to the thermonuclear World War III Jack is always raving about.

I used to think that I was adopted. Or perhaps that the gypsies my grandmother talks about left me on the doorstep. Except gypsies are supposed to be very hot-blooded, too. One thing is for sure: A calm, easygoing person like myself does not belong in this crazy family.

So now you know why sometimes I can't help wishing the Gatemans would adopt me. Especially now, while I am gorging on Mrs. Gatesman's incredible Christmas cookies. My mother's idea of homemade baking is the Pillsbury slice-and-bake cookies from the freezer section of the grocery store. My father is worse: He can't make anything that isn't smothered in tomato sauce.

After we've stuffed ourselves to the point where we feel thoroughly disgusted with ourselves, Tina and I go up to her room. She wants to show me the dress her mother bought her to wear to the New Year's Eve party.

It's rare that Tina and I will be at the same party or dance. Part of it is because, as I explained before, Tina is really involved in band. Also, Tina just doesn't date much. Up until this year she hasn't shown a lot of interest in boys at all. I don't know why, because she's really very attractive.

With me, of course, it's been boys, boys, boys, since I was about ten. Luckily the boys started liking me back not long after that.

The dress looks great on her. She tells me she likes Mike, who is in the same service club as Brian, even though they aren't exactly friends.

"But I'd go with him even if I didn't like him," she confides. "Staying home on New Year's Eve is the pits."

I agree. Last year my old boyfriend and I broke up just before Christmas, and it was probably the worst mistake of my life. I had no date for New Year's Eve, which meant I had no one to kiss at the stroke of midnight. It was depressing. Even if I didn't like him anymore, he would have been better than nothing. Next time I'll wait until after the holidays.

As it turns out, all that worrying about being alone at Simon's house was for nothing. As soon as I'm through the door he tells me he's invited other people over to do a "reading."

"A reading is just what it sounds like," he explains to me while hanging up my coat. "The actors read your play so you can hear how it will sound on stage. It makes it easier to spot the flaws. The dialogue sounds different aloud than it does in your head, you know."

I didn't know, but I could have figured it out. Does he have to be so patronizing?

"Have you thought any about the title change?" he asks.

"Yes." I take a deep breath. "How about *Holden, The Prince of Culpeper County*?"

"I like it," he says, and I nearly faint from the shock. Simon Conreith actually likes something I do?

"Is there really a Culpeper County?"

"Sure there is," I reply in a rush. "Only it's in Virginia. My aunt lives in a neighboring county in a really small town, called Wicksville. Just about everything

20

in that town is called Wicks — Wicks Drug Store, Wicks Garage, Wicks Real Estate — it's like they're the rulers of the town. That's how I got the idea, you see. My hero isn't really a prince, like Hamlet was; it just seems like he is because his family is so important, and he's the only son."

"Good idea." He nods approval, and this time I know I will faint. "You know," he says, leading me into the kitchen, "this play isn't bad. But a lot of the dialogue reads like it's lifted from soap operas or corny Hollywood movies from the fifties."

What can I say? A lot of the dialogue *was* lifted from soap operas and corny movies, the kind of old movies they either show late at night or in the middle of Sunday afternoon. They're usually pretty dumb. I know this. I also know I wouldn't want anyone important to catch me watching them, but I love them all the same. Of course, I'm not going to tell Simon any of this. I just watch him make coffee and keep my mouth shut.

He must have taken my silence for anger, because he immediately adds, "But it's pretty good. A lot better than I expected. I remember you from Mrs. Mason's class last year."

Simon Conreith remembers me? I had barely opened my mouth a dozen times. No one had talked much — except Simon. So what about me had Simon remembered?

I don't have time to ask, even if I had the guts, because the doorbell rings.

Enter Sabrina of the untamed red tresses. She's followed by two other people, but who could notice them behind all that fabulous hair? Beverly and Max are also in the theatrical crowd, but they're, thankfully, a lot less spectacular.

Simon goes back into the kitchen and gets coffee for everyone. This tells you how sophisticated they are. Most teenagers would offer their friends sodas. Or maybe, since it's winter, hot cocoa. There's also the type of guy who would offer his buddies beer — if his parents aren't home. But the *Thespians* drink coffee.

I never drink coffee, because my grandmother drilled it into my head at a very tender age that it would stunt my growth. I don't really believe that, but when you're as short as I am, why take chances?

I also can't stand the taste of it, but I don't tell Simon that. I just put in plenty of milk and sugar. And then I literally force myself to drink it.

"Marie, would you like some coffee with your milk?" Max asks, grinning, and they all smile at his joke. Simon looks at me and frowns.

"Oh, I forgot about you," he says. "Would you prefer a Coke or something?"

"No, this is fine," I assure him, holding onto that mug for dear life.

"You're sure? It's really no problem."

"No, really, I always take my coffee this way." Drinking that coffee-flavored milk has become a point of honor with me. I take a huge swallow and nearly barf right there in the Conreith living room.

At first it's embarrassing listening to them read the lines of my play. It's like someone reading my diary, if I had a diary, that is. But everyone else is so involved that after a while I forget to be embarrassed and start enjoying myself. It's exciting hearing the words I wrote come to life. Simon was right, by the way. Hearing it aloud makes it easy to spot the parts that need to be changed.

If you know the story of *Hamlet*, then you basically know the story of *Holden, The Prince of Culpeper County*. Holden's father has recently died, and his mother remarried his uncle. Holden disapproves of his mother's remarriage, and he really hates his stepfather/uncle, with good reason. Holden has a girlfriend, Opal, whose brother Luke is his best friend. Doing a bit of detective work, Holden finds out that his Uncle Claude killed his father so he could marry his mother and inherit the family fortune. But instead of going to the police or even just killing his stepfather, he goes a little crazy. He drives the people closest to him away — and treats Opal so horribly that she kills herself. In the end he finally does kill Uncle Claude, but it's too late. His whole life is ruined.

I told you it was a tragedy, didn't I?

"This is great," Max says as soon as they're finished reading. "That suicide scene is very powerful."

"And very today, you know, with teen suicide still being a big issue," adds Beverly.

I smile and look modest, but inside I'm feeling *good*. Proud and high as a balloon. They like it! I didn't think I would care so much, but I do.

"It needs work," says Simon, pricking my balloon. "That last scene is particularly awkward. You never explain how Holden finds out his uncle killed his father."

"I don't see that it's necessary," argues Sabrina. "This isn't a whodunit. He's heard a few of the towns-people talking, he's seen his uncle act suspicious — it seems to me he just pieced the information together on his own."

"You couldn't use the ghost, like in the original," Beverly adds. "If someone went around killing people based on what a ghost was telling him, he wouldn't get a lot of sympathy. People would just think he was nuts."

"I adore what you've done with Opal," Sabrina says before Simon can disagree. "She's not a wimp like the original Ophelia."

"She's unsympathetic," Simon pronounces flatly. "When Holden goes to tell her what's been bothering him, she pushes him away. She should be caring and open with him. Instead, she just acts goofy."

They all look at me, and I realize I'm expected to say something. It's like my characters are suddenly on trial, and I'm their defense lawyer.

"Opal acts the way she's been told to act," I say at last. "Her brother was the one to tell her to keep it light and play hard to get. She's afraid to let her real feelings show because she thinks she might lose Holden."

Simon grunts in disbelief. "No girl acts like that these days."

Beverly, Sabrina, and I exchange looks.

"Yeah, but look, Simon," argues Max. "If Holden pours out his heart to Opal, and explains why he's acting so weird, why would she kill herself? She's got to believe his being cruel to her is because he doesn't love her. If she knew about his uncle killing his father, she would forgive his behavior to her. That would ruin the whole thing."

"It needs work," Simon says again, neither disagreeing nor agreeing. "For one thing, the stage directions are sketchy — "

"I thought that was your job," I say.

"It looks like it'll have to be. Listen, I'll just do the necessary changes for you, okay? That'll save us a lot of time and aggravation. Anybody want more coffee?"

"No." Simon looks at me, and I shake my head. "I mean, no, it's not okay with me for you to make the changes. Your job is directing, not writing."

There's a silence in the room and I admit I'm just as surprised as anyone else. Then Simon does his thing with the eyebrow again and shrugs. "I was just trying to save you some work. I thought that was what you'd want."

It might have been what I wanted a few hours ago, but now I knew I'd scratch his eyes out before I'd let him touch one word of my play.

"Thank you," I say as sweetly as I can. "But I think any changes should be done by me. After all, it *is* my play."

"Sure." He shrugs again. "But it'll mean some hard work."

"Fine by me." Oh, if my parents could hear me now! I look him straight in the eyes, not blinking once. "When do we start?"

"After a well-deserved break," Max cuts in. "We've been at this for hours, and I'm starving. Come on, we can discuss it more over a few slices at Pizza Hut."

Everyone falls in with his suggestion, except me. Not because I don't want to — by now I can't imagine anything more appealing than sharing a pizza while discussing my play. But I know Brian is expecting me, and I don't want to keep him waiting too long.

25

"I can't. I've got to go; I'm late as it is," I say regretfully.

"Oh, right," says Simon, and maybe I'm imagining things, but I swear he's sneering. "The boyfriend."

I don't know how to answer this (would you?) so I just say good-bye and leave. I notice no one seems to mind very much. They probably prefer to be by themselves — their own little clique. It's for sure Simon can do without my presence.

Brian's packing in his bedroom when I get to his house, but he comes down, and we go into the kitchen for a Coke.

"How was it?" he asks, sitting down at the kitchen table. "Pretty boring, huh?"

"No, not really. A bunch of the other kids from the drama club came over and they all read my play out loud. It was kind of strange at first, but, Brian, they liked it! All except Simon, of course. That guy is so rude! He thinks everything should be changed, and he wants to do it himself. To save me some work, he says. Can you believe that?"

Brian's back is to me, but he lifts his broad shoulders in a shrug and pours us some more Coke. "Maybe he was just trying to do you a favor."

"No way. He was trying to get rid of me."

"Do you care?" he asks, sitting down next to me. "Why not let the guy do the work if he's so hot to do it? Sounds like a good idea. You don't want to have to put too much time in this thing, do you?"

"Well, not *too* much time," I agree, suddenly tuning into Brian's lack of enthusiasm for this whole thing. Obviously I'm going to have to ease him into it bit by

26

bit. "But it *is* my play. I don't want him hacking it to pieces."

"Yeah, I guess you're right." He scoots his chair closer to mine and puts his arm around my shoulder. "I just haven't gotten used to the idea yet."

Didn't I tell you he was nice? "That makes two of us," I tell him. "But enough about that — are you all ready to hit the slopes tomorrow?"

"You bet. My dad's been listening to the snow reports all day. I can't wait to try out my new boots. I just wish you were going to be with us."

There's nothing on earth that would get me on a ski slope. Skiing, in my mind, ranks along with skydiving and car racing as the most dangerous and least fun sports ever invented. I figure anyone who steps into a pair of skis has to have some kind of a death wish. But I don't tell Brian any of this. I cuddle closer until I can hear his heart beating through his shirt, and the little silver necklace dangles between us.

"Me, too," I lie. "But at least we'll be together for the New Year's Eve party."

"Yeah, that should be a blast. I promise not to break any bones."

Brian keeps his promise; he doesn't break any bones, but he does manage to sprain his wrist. He's not too upset about it, because he figures it's going to get him out of a lot of written assignments. Actually, if it weren't for the fact that he also can't drive, he'd be delirious with joy.

We go to the party anyway, getting a ride with Brian's best friend, Josh, and his girlfriend, Ashley. Brian looks very dashing and heroic in his sling, and he gets to tell his story several times. That brings the conversation in our group around to accidents, and the guys try to outdo each other with gruesome tales of paralyzed people and dismembered body parts. Kind of a grim way to start the new year, if you know what I mean.

Then the talk gets around to my play, and I have to explain the plot to everybody.

"How does the hero kill his uncle?" one of Brian's jock friends asks.

"He strangles him."

"Wicked! Does the uncle go like this?"

He puts his hands around his neck and makes these gross choking noises.

"Something like that," I agree. "Only not so authentic."

Everybody else seems more concerned with Opal's suicide. I think they call this morbid curiosity. The guys all think it's corny, but the girls are asking question like they think it's romantic.

"Do you have anyone to play Opal yet?" Ashley asks, and I shake my head.

"Auditions begin next week."

"You know, I've been thinking about auditioning," Ashley says, and everyone, including her boyfriend, turns and looks at her in astonishment. "That role sounds perfect for me, don't you think?"

"I didn't know you were into acting," I say.

"I never thought much about it before. But like, ever since I heard you wrote it, I've been thinking about it a lot. Like maybe acting would make a good career for me. I have some experience, you know."

Oh, God, I think. She's not going to mention the sunflower thing again, is she?

"You remember," she says chidingly. "In elementary school. I was the sunflower in the first-grade play."

I do remember. But I wouldn't exactly call it acting experience. All she had to do was move around a little bit and say one or two lines about the sun. That didn't make her Meryl Streep. Especially since she only got the part because she was tall and had blonde hair.

"And then I was the princess in second grade," she continues.

She got that part basically because her mother bought the costume. Also, let's face it, she's pretty. She was always pretty. And even in second grade she looked like a princess.

"Well, sure I remember," I tell her. "You were great! Both times!"

"I don't know, babe," Josh says doubtfully. "That girl sure sounds loony to me. But if that's what you want — " Josh gives me a big smile. "Why can't our playwright arrange it for you?"

"Oh, I don't have anything to do with auditions," I put in quickly. "You should talk to Simon or Mr. Phillips, Ashley."

"But they'd listen to you," Ashley says. "Couldn't you, like, put in a word for me?"

"Sure she could," says a voice next to me, and I realize it belongs to Brian. "Right, Marie?"

He puts his arm around me. I look out into a sea of faces and get this sinking feeling. I'm trapped. What can I do? I don't want those faces to turn unfriendly.

"I'll do what I can," I promise. "But you know,

Ashley, this is really a man's play. Even Opal's part isn't that large."

"There are no small parts, only small actors," she replies. "I heard that once on *Entertainment Tonight*."

"Hey, Marie, if it's a man's play, how about giving me a chance?" Josh shouts, standing up on one of the chairs. " 'To be or not to be'," he begins, with his hand over his heart, and everybody starts booing.

Josh improvises the rest, since that's all he knows of Hamlet's famous soliloquy. His jokes are really awful, but everybody cracks up, even me. Only I'm laughing because I'm imagining the look on Simon's face if he could hear Josh murder Shakespeare. He'd be so horrified that he'd probably have a stroke.

Of course, even if he did, that still wouldn't guarantee Ashley the part of Opal.

A few minutes later I'm hiding out in the bathroom with Tina — it's the first time I've had the chance to talk to her all evening.

"What am I going to do, Tina?" I ask frantically, watching her in the mirror as she fixes her face for the main event at midnight. I'm so stressed out I don't even bother to comb my hair. "They all think I can get her the role. Unless you count the flower bit and the time she strutted around the stage in that pink princess getup, she's never acted in her life!"

"Sure she has. Just not on stage." Tina does a pout into the mirror and flips her hair in perfect imitation of Ashley. Laughing takes my mind off the problem for exactly two seconds before I start to worry again.

Ashley is sort of a friend of mine, and I do like her, even though she is a little hard to take at times. Also she's a cheerleader, very popular, and not someone you want to cross. Not that she's mean or anything like that. She doesn't need to be. She can make life miserable for you just by not speaking to you. That's the kind of power she has. Naturally all the boys in our school think she's the greatest thing since MTV.

"Come on, Tina. Tell me what I'm going to do."

"Do what you said you'd do. Talk to Simon."

The thought is enough to curl my toes. I shake my head. "Simon will never agree to it."

"Okay. But he has to give her an audition like everyone else, doesn't he? Just make sure it's Simon who gives her the thumbs down."

"I'll still get blamed." I sigh, pushing my hair back from my face. "Why does everything have to be so complicated?"

"You worry too much," Tina says, studying her face critically in the mirror. "What do you think? More blush?"

"Not unless you're trying out for the circus. You look great, honestly," I tell her. "I'm the one who needs a major overhaul. Look at me; I'm a zombie! Hand me some of that blush, will you?" I lean closer to the mirror and start pinching my cheeks. "I wonder what Simon is doing tonight?"

Tina stops, gives me this funny look, and then scrunches up her mouth the way she does when she's thinking. "Let's see . . . he's sitting before a blazing fire, reading romantic poetry, and sipping capuccino. He's wearing a black cashmere sweater and tight jeans that are *to die*, and his faithful Irish setter is curled up at his feet."

"No date?" I ask, mentally replacing the Irish setter

with Sabrina. Not that Sabrina's a dog, but if she were, she'd be something classy like an Irish setter. And I could definitely see Sabrina and Simon reading love sonnets together.

"Of course he has a date — it's New Year's Eve! Let's see, she's an older, sophisticated woman, a graduate student in nineteenth-century Russian literature or something like that. Right now she's in the other room, slipping into something more comfortable." Tina smiles. "Why do you care, anyway?"

"I don't. I was just wondering, that's all."

She catches my eye in the mirror, and then we both break into a fit of giggles. Someone chooses that moment to start pounding on the door. There are three girls waiting in line, and they give us dirty looks as we leave.

"What's their problem?" Tina asks. "There are at least six bathrooms in this house."

"It's not a house, it's a mausoleum. The kid who lives here must have rich parents."

"I've got to find Mike," Tina says, standing on tiptoe and looking over heads. "He's probably wondering what took me so long."

"I'd better get back, too," I say, looking in the other direction. "Talk to you later."

"Much later. Like next year."

She goes back to Mike, and I go back to Brian, which isn't easy because there are a lot of people in the room, comparing the second hands of their watches. I practically have to fight my way through the crowd.

I feel a little better after talking with Tina, even if it was for only a few minutes in the bathroom. And her advice is good. All I have to do is make sure Simon is the one who comes out as the bad guy. That shouldn't be too hard.

I wish Brian and I could double-date with Tina and Mike. It would be a nice change from Josh and Ashley and the rest of Brian's friends. Brian wouldn't see it that way, of course, but I'll find some way to convince him to at least give it a try. I know Brian and Mike would hit it off given half the chance, and then I'd get to see more of Tina.

I make a note in my head to talk to Brian about it later. After all, why should we have to go out with Brian's friends all the time and never mine?

Three

I get sick just before Christmas vacation ends and spend the first two days of school in bed with a horrible cold. My catching a cold just before I have to see Simon and ask him about Ashley proves that sickness can be brought about by emotional stress. Obviously my body wants to put off that day just as much as the rest of me does.

On the third day I rise from the dead, feeling about as bad as the weather, today being your average bleak and dreary January morning. I somehow manage to get dressed and straggle into school, still weak and sucking down Smith Brothers' cough drops like they're candy, which I guess they pretty much are.

The first thing I see when I get to school is a notice for auditions for *Holden, The Prince of Culpeper County*. Now it's official, I think. There is no turning back.

I feel half excited, half scared, like the way you feel the first time a boy kisses you. You want to, but you're not sure it's going to come out right. I mean, you start thinking that your noses are going to bump, or that your breath smells of whatever you had for dinner, or that maybe you'll accidentally drip saliva or something disgusting like that. You see, by now I want to see my play on stage, only I'm afraid it's going to be a major disaster. Just like my first kiss with Bucky Frischman.

After school I have to meet you-know-who in the drama room. Simon is still dying to get his greedy little hands on my script and change it past all recognition. But today I just don't have the engery to give him much of a fight.

"I talked over Opal's suicide with Mr. Phillips," he says first thing, not even asking me how I feel when it must be obvious I'm not feeling one hundred percent. "I think I've figured out the solution."

"I didn't know there was a problem." Wearily I open another box of cough drops. I can see this is going to take a while. "Everybody else seemed to really like it."

"Yeah, basically it's good," he says, waving his hand. "But it's not explained enough. The real drama and excitement of the scene is lost because she does it *offstage*."

"Well, it's kind of hard to show someone drowning herself in a river *onstage*, isn't it? You couldn't get a tub of water big enough." I pause. "Oh, do you want her to kill herself some other way, because if you do — "

"No, no, the river is great. But we don't need real water. Picture this: We get huge pieces of blue material, something shiny like silk, or some kind of material like that, and then we flutter it across the stage, so it looks like water — get it?" Simon starts moving his hands like a wave.

"Where would we get this material?" I ask. After all, one of us has to be practical. This is Magothy Senior High we are dealing with, not Broadway. "What holds the material in place?"

"Oh, we'd get it from some fabric store," he says carelessly. "And people would hold it on either side, simulating waves, like this — " Again he starts with the wave motions. "And then Opal would walk into the water, like she's in a trance, slowly letting it engulf her."

"Gee, I don't know. It sounds kind of complicated. Are you sure we could carry it off?"

"Absolutely. Oh, another thing — she'll be talking to herself as she goes in, letting the audience know for sure that she's totally lost her mind."

"More dialogue?" My heart sinks fast. "Oh, God, you don't want her to sing, do you?" In the original, the mad Ophelia goes around the court singing weird songs. There I draw the line. I'm no good at music and I hate rhymes. I am definitely not going to write a song.

"No, she'll be muttering things that Holden has said to her — for instance, when he says he loves her, and then when he says he hates her, she just repeats them over and over again — "

"Oh, I see. So we just have her muttering crazily, using some of Holden's lines." Lines already written. Good. No extra work for me.

"Right. And then she meets her watery grave."

He utters the last very dramatically, and any other

time I would laugh, only I've caught some of his enthusiasm. I try to picture the scene the way he described it, and I have to admit, the picture in my head is better than the one I wrote.

"I like it . . . I like it," I tell him and take out a sheet of paper. "We could use that blue material at the end, too, when Holden strangles his uncle. Instead of being near the water, they'll be right in it — what do you think?"

"I think it's a great idea. Let's get to it."

I write, we discuss, then we discuss, and I write for I don't know how long. By the time we're finished my fingers are cramped and the muscles in my neck are sore. But it works. Opal's scene, that is. I can see that Simon's way is really going to increase the audience's sympathy for Opal, just like he says.

"That's good. Really good," nods Simon, reading it over, and then he *smiles* at me. No kidding. And what a smile! I never noticed before how white and even his teeth are, and how he has one dimple on the left side of his mouth. The effect is enough to take your breath away, honestly.

"You should do that more often," I murmur, speaking my thoughts aloud without really intending to. The minute the words leave my mouth, I want to die. What an incredibly dumb thing to say!

The smile vanishes, and he looks at me blankly. "What?"

"Never mind." I shake my head. "Was there anything else you wanted to discuss?"

"Uh — oh, right, the big love scene," he says decisively, turning the pages of his script until he gets to the part he wants. " 'I've loved you since we were

37

kids together,' " he reads. " 'I need you, sweetheart. Please don't leave me — ' "

"That's okay, you don't need to read the whole thing," I interrupt hastily. "What's the matter with it?"

"It doesn't flow right. Holden does all the talking. All Opal says is 'I love you, too.' She needs to express her feelings more."

"I didn't want to get too mushy, in case Mr. Phillips thought . . . well, you know what I mean." One look at his face and it's obvious he has no idea what I mean. I squirm, feeling about as mature as a six-year-old. It's really embarrassing to be embarrassed by something when the other person isn't. Why does Simon always have to act so sophisticated? Why can't he act like any other normal teenage boy?

"Everybody will laugh at that part as it is," I finish lamely.

"Only morons will laugh."

"Oh, I don't know about that. My friends will probably laugh."

Simon raises one black eyebrow in reply. Darn it! I walked right into that one.

"The point is," he continues, "if the audience doesn't have a clear understanding of the depth of her emotions, then they won't understand why she goes crazy enough to kill herself."

The depth of her emotions? That just goes to show you that Simon is not your average boy. Where did he learn to talk like that? "Okay," I mutter, popping another cough drop into my dry mouth and massaging my sore neck muscles. "I'll work on it, and get it to you by Friday. Promise."

He wants more emotion? I'll give him more emotion. I haven't spent all those afternoons in front of the TV watching *Santa Barbara* for nothing. I'll write a scene so drippy and gooey that even Mr. Totally Unfazeable will blush.

Thinking of ways to get back at Simon must have given me a weird expression, because suddenly he is looking at me strangely.

"Are you feeling all right, Marie?" he asks, peering into my face, like he's seeing for the first time that it's blotchy and red and that my nose is peeling from so much sneezing. "You don't look so hot."

"Thanks for noticing." Like I need him to tell me how terrible I look. "It's just a cold."

"I'd better drive you home."

"Oh, that's all right," I say, startled. From what I know of Simon, I'd say his acts of kindness toward those he considers his intellectual inferiors are few and far between. "Thanks anyway."

"Your boyfriend waiting for you?"

"No, but I can take the activity bus."

"It's left by now," he says, looking at his watch. "We went on later than I expected. Come on, I don't mind dropping you off. You're not even out of my way."

So we gather up our books, bundle up into our coats, scarves, and gloves, and trudge out into the parking lot.

I'm expecting Simon to drive something sleek and classy, and black, of course. But Simon's car is as individualistic as he is; a beat-up old clunker painted bright turquoise. No fooling, it looks like a gigantic turquoise bomb.

"Doesn't get very good mileage, but she's got char-acter, doesn't she?" Simon asks.

She? "Oh, yes," I agree hastily. "And colorful . . . you couldn't lose it in a parking lot."

"Yeah, they don't make them like this anymore."

Thank you, Mr. Ford, I think to myself as I scramble into the car. I have to get in on the driver's side because the door on the passenger side is broken. But at least the heater works. In the dead of winter that's about all that matters, in my opinion.

Simon, I notice, starts heading in the general di-rection of my house, without my telling him what the general direction is. When I gave him my address he seems to know where it is, even though we don't ex-actly live on the main drag. And, for the record, he doesn't live that close to me. As a matter of fact, I am definitely out of the way for him. But the car is warm, and he says he doesn't mind. Why complain?

Simon starts talking about the auditions, and I re-alize it's now or never if I'm going to put in a good word for Ashley.

"I guess you have some idea of who you want in each part already," I begin tentatively.

He shrugs. "There will be some regulars at the au-ditions, but I think we'll get a lot of first-timers, too. I'm sure we'll have a lot of good people to choose from. This all-student production has been getting a lot of attention, you know."

Did I ever — I was in the thick of it, so to speak. "Have you thought about who would be good for the part of Opal?"

"I can't say for sure yet, but Sabrina will be giving

40

the others some stiff competition. I read some of the scenes with her, and she's good."

The love scenes, I'm sure. So *that's* how he knew they were too short!

"Don't you think that's maybe giving her an unfair advantage?"

"Maybe." He gives me a sidelong glance, and there's the tiniest hint of a smile. "But Mr. Phillips gets final say, you know."

"I have a friend trying out for Opal," I tell him, gathering up my courage. "You probably know her."

"Who is it?"

"Ashley Hutton."

"Oh, the cheerleader," he says, like cheerleaders are some sort of lower life form. "Does she have any experience?"

Dare I mention the sunflower and fairy princess? No, better not. "Well, not exactly," I hedge, and Simon just grunts.

"Figures."

"Does every cast member have to be a member of your little clique?" I demand.

"No, they only have to be good. So don't expect Ashley to get preferential treatment just because she's a friend of yours. She gets the same chance everybody else does, and that's it."

"Well, fine. As long as it's a fair one." The look he throws me is positively chilling, and too late I realize that getting Simon angry isn't going to do Ashley any good. "Which I'm sure it will be," I add placatingly, but Simon doesn't seem to hear me. Our brief moments of shared camaraderie are definitely over.

We drive the rest of the way in silence. Simon pulls into my driveway and stops so fast I have to hold on to my seat. He gets out of the car, barely giving me time to scoot out before getting in again.

"Hope you feel better," he mutters, slamming the door.

"Thanks for dropping me off," I say brightly, but he doesn't hear me. He's already in reverse.

I watch the turquoise bomb peel out with the terrible knowledge that Ashley has about as much chance of getting the part of Opal as I do of winning the women's decathlon in the next Olympics. Even if she turns out to be good, unlikely as that possibility is, Simon is sure to hold a grudge against her because of me. I've *doomed* her.

All of which means she'll get mad at me. And then her boyfriend — Brian's best friend, if you remember — will get mad at me. And then Brian will get mad at me. That will be four people, including Simon, who will be mad at me, and just because I tried to do a friend a favor. To tell you the truth, I don't even like Ashley all that much.

My boots make crunchy noises through the snow as I make my way slowly up to our house. If only this cold would turn into double pneumonia, I think, looking at the thick white blanket covering our lawn. I wonder if I could get really ill if I spent the rest of the afternoon making angels in the snow. Or maybe I could just go to the local hospital and ask some very sick people to breathe on me.

I really don't want to go to that audition.

• • •

Simon, of course, assigns the most difficult scene for each audition. That means that the boys trying out for Holden will have to read the scene where he confronts his mother, and that the girls trying out for Opal will have to read the scene where she kills herself.

Ashley's not too happy about this. She tells me so when I go over to her house the day before the auditions to help her in any way I can. She's not too shaken by the complexity of the scene; she just doesn't like the idea that she has to appear with her hair messed up, looking bedraggled.

"Can't she just take some pills?" she asks me very seriously, and I sigh.

"No, Ashley, that wouldn't be as dramatic."

"Oh, well," she says airily. "Maybe we can work out something with Simon."

My head snaps up. I don't like the sound of that. She hasn't even got the part and already she's manipulating the director. Besides, here is the great emotional scene I'd poured my heart into, and she's worried about her hair! I swear, if she weren't Brian's best friend's girlfriend and the most popular girl in school, I'd tell her to forget it. She just doesn't have the right attitude to play Opal.

Only she *is* Brian's best friend's girlfriend and the most popular girl in school. Enough said?

"Let's try it again," I tell her. "This time you might want to remember that her mental state is really bad when she decides to go into the river. She's totally lost it, you know?"

"I still don't see why she just can't, like, take some

pills. And why does she have to die before the end of the play?"

Luckily, I don't have to answer that because the doorbell rings.

"That'll be Josh and Brian," Ashley says, tossing the script on the table. "I told them to stop by after they were finished skating."

Not only Josh and Brian, but a whole bunch from our gang troop in, laughing, talking, their faces still red from the cold. We all go down to the basement to listen to Ashley's new CD player.

"Josh wanted me to ask you if you talked to that Simon guy about Ashley," Brian says, drawing me aside.

"Well, yes, I did, but I don't think I did any good. He made it very clear that he won't give her any special treatment. Everything depends upon the audition."

Brian frowns. "So how did it go this afternoon?"

"To tell you the truth," I answer carefully, "I don't think Ashley has the right attitude to play Opal, and I'm afraid that's going to hurt her chances tomorrow."

Brian's eyes follow mine to where Ashley is handing out drinks to everybody. "She doesn't look worried," he says. "Besides, she's pretty enough for the part. None of the other girls can touch her."

"There's more to Opal than just being pretty," I say sharply, and Brian turns to me in surprise.

"Hey, you're not jealous, are you? This is a first!" His face lights up and he puts his arms around me.

"No, of course I'm not — "

"Because you know I think you're pretty, too, Marie," he says, nuzzling my ear. "I always have. You have nothing to worry about on that score."

I sigh. The fact that Ashley is prettier than me is not exactly shocking news. Ashley is prettier than Miss America. But being jealous of Ashley is about the last thing I'm feeling right now. I'd like to explain this to Brian, but I figure, why bother? The idea of me being jealous seems to make him very happy.

Is it any wonder that I'm practically a basket case by the time I get home? Between fending off Brian, who has suddenly become an octopus, and worrying about the auditions, is it any wonder that I have no appetite for dinner, even though it's my favorite — lasagna?

Not that Mom and Dad notice that I'm not really with it. They're having another one of their disagreements. This time it's about the new tax laws. Mom starts it innocently enough by commenting that they're not going to get as big a refund from the government as they did in previous years. Dad agrees it's a shame, and then starts going on about how it's about time corporate America started paying their fair share, and how big businesses use loopholes so that they hardly have to pay any taxes at all.

Mom, who works for a big corporation, gets that telltale gleam in her eye. At this point I start muttering about having to get to my homework.

"But, Marie, honey, you haven't even touched your dinner," Mom exclaims before I can make good my escape. "Are you coming down with another cold?"

"No, I'm just tired."

"You've been working hard," Dad comments, the tax injustices suffered by the working class momentarily forgotten. "Don't think your mother and I

45

haven't noticed. We want you to know that we're very proud of you." He beams at me, ruffling my hair, which I positively cannot stand. "Aren't we, Kathleen?"

"Yes," my mother nods, frowning, "but we don't want you making yourself sick. Are you sure there isn't something worrying you, Marie?"

"I guess I'm kind of keyed up about the auditions tomorrow."

"Such problems!" Dad exclaims. "Anyone would think you were auditioning!"

God forbid. Don't I have enough to worry about? "I just wish I didn't have to be there."

"Of course you want to be there," Mom gasps. "After all, it's your play."

"Your mother's right, honey. Some of the decision should be yours."

"Mr. Phillips is the one who makes the final decision. Or maybe Simon will. He's so bossy he'll probably overrule even Mr. Phillips."

"Has that boy been giving you trouble?" my mother demands. "Don't you let him steamroll you, Marie. You have just as much right to be a part of the decision-making process as he does. More, come to think of it. After all, what is he? Just the *director*!"

The way she says it, you'd think the director's importance was several notches lower than that of the guy who hands out programs. But that's one thing I forgot to mention about my mother. On political and economic issues she's very conservative, but when it comes to women's rights, you don't want to mess with her. My brother Jack told me once it's because she had such a hard time herself as a woman lawyer.

"I think it's customary, Kathleen," my father says

tentatively, "for the director to pick the cast."

"Why, because he's a *man*? Marie wrote the play, Frank. I'm sure she has definite ideas on who should play the characters."

"Actually — " I begin, but my mother cuts me right off.

"I don't want my daughter thinking it's acceptable to play second fiddle to some *boy* just because she's a girl. Marie has got to start being assertive now. If she's ever going to get anywhere in this male-dominated world, she's got to learn to stick up for herself and not to take any garbage from men!"

"Whoa, Kathleeen," my father interrupts, and I have to give him credit for having guts. And stupidity. You'd think he'd know by now this is one argument he can't win.

"I'm sure Marie will find a different world when she gets out of college than the one you found," he says. "Things have changed in the last twenty years for women, certainly much faster than they have for other minorities. When I think of — "

I don't stay for Dad's reminiscences of the Civil Rights Movement. (Would you?) They barely notice when I get up to go to my room, which is pretty strange if you consider that their discussion started over me.

I lay on my bed and reach for the phone to call Tina. I have to talk to somebody. By now I really, really, *really* don't want to go to that audition.

Four

"Next, please," Mr. Phillips calls from his chair, and another Holden hopeful takes the stage. His name is Adam Cooke; he's a senior, on the tennis team, and cute, although he doesn't fit my image of what Holden should look like. Adam's the last to audition, and I'm hoping he'll be better than the guys before him.

There isn't anyone left to try out for Grace, Holden's mother, so Mr. Phillips asks Sabrina to step in. Adam, who looked nervous before, now looks near death. I guess it's daunting enough to have to read this really heavy scene without having to do it with Magothy High's leading lady.

Sabrina, of course, takes it in stride. She flashes him an encouraging smile, and that seems to relax him a bit. He even manages a weak smile back.

"Okay, people, you know where to start. Whenever you're ready," says Mr. Phillips.

Sabrina waits a few moments, then asks gently, "What's wrong with you, honey?"

Adam takes a big breath and holds it. Nothing. Sabrina tries again. "What's wrong with you, honey?"

"What's wrong?" he demands in a rush, his voice cracking a little at the end. "You ask me what's wrong? Not six months after your husband's death you marry his brother, and you ask me what's wrong! What's wrong is living here and having to see you kissing and caring for that murderer! That slimy weasel! That snake in the grass!"

"Holden!" Sabrina says sharply. "You are speaking to your mother!"

"I'm speaking to the woman who has made a Sodom and Gomorrah out of my father's house! You've blackened our family's name! You're not worth the dirt my father walked on!"

"Stop it, stop it, stop it!" Sabrina shrieks and slaps him across the face.

I told you it was heavy, didn't I?

Adam looks stunned for a moment before going on. I don't think he was prepared for a real slap. But it seems to help his acting; either that or he really is angry at Sabrina. He looks like he's just dying to hit her back.

Adam turns in a pretty good performance. Sabrina, not even trying, is better. When she reads Opal, the part she is trying out for, she's super. I don't see how anyone could top her.

Ashley, worse luck, has to follow Sabrina, and by comparison, she's a total disaster.

"He loves me, he loves me not," she says tonelessly, picking the petals off a daisy. "He said he loved me. 'I've always loved you, Opal.' Uh — uh — "

" 'Ever since we were kids together,' " prompts Simon.

"What?"

" 'Ever since we were kids together!' " everybody says in unison, and Ashley gives Simon a very un-Opal-like smile.

"Thanks. 'Ever since we were kids together, I've loved you — ' " Simon gives me this sneering look, and I sink lower into my chair. Why couldn't Ashley be satisfied with being a cheerleader and the most popular girl at Magothy High?

There are two more girls after Ashley, neither one much better. The last one to audition is the kind of girl you wouldn't give a second glance. Small, like me, but with washed-out looks and a timid voice. She walks on stage and announces she's new to Magothy, a sophomore, and that her name is Deirdre Lamb.

Mr. Phillips sighs like he wishes he didn't even have to bother. He, like Simon, is set on Sabrina.

"Go ahead, Denise," calls Mr. Phillips.

"That's Deirdre."

"Oh — fine, whenever you're ready."

Deirdre stands perfectly still for a moment, closing her eyes tightly before opening them again. That's when the amazing transformation takes place. I don't know how to describe it except to say that Deirdre, small and inconspicuous, suddenly *becomes* Opal.

Mr. Phillips looks as surprised as when he first found out I wrote the play. That should teach him to judge people solely on appearances! When she's finished he's silent for a moment.

"Excellent, De — "

"Deirdre," Simon whispers to him.

"Yes, yes, excellent, my dear. Adam, would you read with Deirdre, please?"

Adam steps on stage. He doesn't look so nervous to be acting with Deirdre as he did with Sabrina, but then, he doesn't look so thrilled, either.

"Do you know you're absolutely beautiful?" he says.

"Yes, I've heard that before," she replies, tilting her head flirtatiously.

"Do you also know that I'm crazy about you and the sight of you with all these other men makes me mad with jealousy?"

"How mad?"

"So mad my blood boils, and I want to kick their teeth out so they can never smile at you again."

"You always did have a way about you, Holden," she says, sighing, and it's a real *Opal* sigh. It's as if Deirdre got into my head and knows exactly how Opal is supposed to act and talk.

The auditions are over with pretty shortly after that. Mr. Phillips tells everyone they were fantastic and that the final decisions will be posted outside the auditorium tomorrow afternoon.

After everyone leaves, Mr. Phillips starts discussing the possibilities with us. In no time at all he and Simon decide on most of the cast. I don't have much to say.

"Adam Cooke was the best Holden," says Simon.

51

"I think he could be improved with some work."

"He'll need it," agrees Mr. Phillips. "Any objections, Marie?"

I shake my head.

"Okay, then, now to the women. Who do you see for Opal, Marie?"

"Oh, gee, I don't know," I say weakly.

"But surely you must have some opinion," Mr. Phillips prods.

"Well," I clear my throat. I *have* to say something for Ashley, don't I? "Well," I repeat. "I thought Ashley looked pretty good."

"Are you out of your mind?" Simon roars. "She was terrible!"

"Well, not all terrible. I happen to think there were some good points in her performance."

"Name one!" Simon challenges, and now I am really squirming. Even Mr. Phillips is looking at me strangely. Desperately I search for something nice to say about Ashley.

"Well, she's got the right hair color, for instance."

"Of all the stupid remarks you've ever made, and you've made plenty of them, that's about the stupidest!" Simon exclaims. "What does her hair color have to do with it, for crying out loud?"

"I've always pictured Opal as a blonde."

"Did you also picture her delivering her lines with the depth and emotion of a wooden spoon? Admit it, you just want her because she's a friend of yours!"

"Hey, hey — break it up, you two," Mr. Phillips says. "Discussion is healthy, but let's try to be professional, shall we? Simon, why don't you tell us who you think should get the role."

"Yeah, give us your *unbiased* opinion," I say sarcastically.

"Deirdre," Simon replies, and my mouth drops open in amazement. "She's perfect for the part," he says. "She has that wraith-like appearance, the vulnerability of Opal. She's exactly how I envision the role."

"Not Sabrina?" Mr. Phillips asks, which is exactly what I'm wondering.

Simon shakes his head. "Sabrina is too vivid, too alive. Actually, I see Sabrina as Grace. There was great tension between Sabrina and Adam — I picked up on it right away."

Mr. Phillips nods his head thoughtfully. "Good choice, Simon. Well, you two, that's all for today. I expect you to keep this discussion between yourselves — we don't want to create any hard feelings, do we?"

Simon gives me a thunderous look. Too late, Mr. Phillips, I think. The hard feelings are already created.

As soon as Mr. Phillips leaves, Simon turns on me like a snarling dog. Honestly, he all but bares his teeth at me.

"Okay, okay, you're right. I was wrong," I tell him before he can chew me out. "Just don't get bent out of shape, okay?"

"I knew you were an airhead, but you are totally *unreal*," he says, ignoring my plea for peace. "You really don't care about this play, do you? You don't care about anything at all!"

"Of course I care!" I protest. "Didn't I spend practically the whole week working on the love scene you didn't think was good enough?"

"Yeah, and then you're prepared to throw all that

work away by giving the part of Opal to *Ashley*! Ashley's a zero; you know that as well as I do, yet you're willing to put her in a pivotal role — sabotage your own play — just to please her!"

"If you remember correctly, I didn't say I thought Ashley should get the role," I say with some difficulty. "I just said that there were some good things about her performance."

"You don't believe that any more than I do," he says, with a snort of disgust. "Man, have I lost total respect for you, Marie. You're nothing more than a phony! A shallow, superficial phony!"

"I am not!"

"Yeah, that's exactly what you are. But you'd better get your act together or get out of this thing, because none of this garbage cuts it with me. This production is the biggest thing that's ever happened to the Thespians, and it's my first chance to direct! I'm not going to let you blow it!"

And then he storms out.

For a moment I just stand there, sort of numb. There's a big ache inside the wall of my chest and behind my eyes, the way it aches when you want to cry, but can't, or won't. I won't. I won't let Simon make me cry. I won't let him matter so much.

I can't believe he said those things to me! Why does he have to be so mean? Why can't he understand that it isn't easy for me, either?

I walk out into the parking lot — luckily I have Mom's car today. Once inside the car, I have to take several deep breaths, because I'm shaking. I try to put the key into the ignition. It won't fit. I ram it in again and again until I'm about ready to scream, and then

I realize that it's the trunk key. I get the right key in and start the car.

"I'm not going to let anything that jerk said upset me," I say loudly to myself, leaving the parking lot. In the car next to me I see a man look at me uncertainly, like he's not sure, but he thinks I might be a lunatic. I avert my face and pretend I'm listening to the radio.

"Who does he think he is, anyway?" I ask and then stomp on the brakes as I narrowly avoid sideswiping a car. The blue-haired old lady driving it gives me a nasty look over the steering wheel and honks her horn really loud, three times. I can feel all the other drivers turn to look at me. After that I stop talking to myself and concentrate on getting home in one piece.

I'm still shaking when I finally get to the safety of my room. I immediately call Tina. The line is busy. I try again and again and am still trying when Mom calls me to dinner.

"I'm not hungry!" I shout. "Go ahead without me!"

"What, again?" I hear my father ask her. "What does she mean she's not hungry?"

I don't hear my mother's reply, but my father's booming voice comes across loud and clear. "What do you think? Is she on some sort of crazy diet? Maybe this is a warning sign for anorexia? Kathleen, I don't like this. She's got to eat something. Marie!" he yells, and I sigh.

"All right, I'm coming," I yell back.

For all this commotion you might think dinner is something really special, instead of cold cuts and assorted goodies from the deli. They didn't even bother to take it out of the containers, for Pete's sake.

"What's the matter, Marie?" my father asks. "Those auditions didn't go well?"

"They were fine."

"Are you pleased with the cast?" asks my mother.

I shrug. "Yeah, they're okay."

There's a silence, and I can sense Mom and Dad are practicing that unspoken communication parents are so good at. You know, where they look at each other and signal like mad with their eyes.

"Mom," I blurt out, "do you think I'm superficial?"

"Why, no," she says, surprised. "No," she repeats more firmly. "At least not in the modern usage of the word. You've never been one to make too much over your appearance like so many girls your age."

I think about this for a moment. "What about shallow? Do you think I'm shallow?"

"Shallow? Oh, no, not really, Marie. I admit you're not as committed to the important issues as your father and I would like, but now we see that your passion is going to be your writing. And that's just wonderful. We're tremendously pleased about that, aren't we, Frank?"

Dad nods. "I only wish we'd seen it sooner."

"But we knew it was just a matter of time before you found your niche," adds Mom. "We knew that sooner or later you'd find something to care about — and you have!"

I wince. Somehow this is not making me feel better the way I'd hoped.

Dad's forehead wrinkles in a suspicious frown. "Did you have a fight with Brian?" he demands. "Is that what this is all about? Listen to me, sweetheart, that's the oldest trick in the book — "

"Oh, *Dad*," I groan, standing up. "You've got it all wrong. It isn't Brian. It's me!"

I go back upstairs and turn on my stereo so I can't hear them discussing me. I call Tina again. This time I reach her house, but her sister tells me she isn't home. Darn!

I'm in the bathroom some minutes later when I hear the phone ring. Dad gets to it before I can.

"You want to speak to my daughter?" I hear him snarl into the receiver. "Well, Brian, I'm not sure that's a good — "

"I'm here, Dad," I say breathlessly into my extension. "You can hang up now, I've got it." There is silence. "*Dad*," I repeat patiently. "I said you can *hang up now*."

Dad hangs up the phone with extreme reluctance.

"What's with him?" Brian asks. "Jeez, he acted like I was a murderer or something."

"Oh, you know, bad day at the office," I lie.

"Yeah, mine has those, too. Hey, are we still getting together to study tonight?"

"Oh, gee, I almost forgot." I look down at the script sitting on my desk. "Listen, Brian, would you mind terribly if we didn't?"

"No — you okay, Marie?"

My fingers curl around the edges of the script, and I debate whether I should tell him or not. He might make me feel better. I know for sure that Brian doesn't think I'm a phony or superficial or shallow or any of those horrible things Simon said to me.

"I'm fine," I say finally. "Except I've got a headache."

"Oh. Well, take two aspirin and call me in the

morning," he jokes, then says more seriously, "I hope you feel better, Marie."

Isn't he the sweetest guy ever? "Thanks," I mumble, and lay the receiver back in its cradle.

Why didn't I tell him the truth? That I'm not fine, that it isn't just a headache? Why didn't I tell him about my fight with Simon?

Feel better.

I lie across the bed and start thinking about the auditions. About how Simon spoke so strongly for Deirdre, even though Sabrina is his friend, maybe even his girlfriend. He wasn't worried that Sabrina would be mad at him. He did what was best for the play.

Which is more than I did.

Maybe he's right. Maybe I am all those things he said I am.

I pick up the script and begin to leaf through it. Words I wrote leap off the page at me. Words and lines actors would soon be bringing to life.

"I do care," I say aloud. "I do care."

Five

"Honestly, I didn't have anything to do with the final decision," I'm telling Ashley for about the hundredth time during lunch two days later. The cast list was posted yesterday, and now a bunch of us are sitting at the Pizza Parlor, trying to cheer Ashley up. She's having none of it; she just sits there and sulks, toying tragically with her food.

"I spoke up for you, Ashley," I defend myself. "But they were really set on Deirdre."

"Who is this Deirdre, anyway?" Brian asks. "I never even heard of her."

"She's a nothing," replies Josh. "A double bagger."

This, of course, is an exaggeration. Deirdre might not have Ashley's spectacular looks, but she isn't ugly. I clear my throat.

"She's new to Magothy Beach," I tell Brian. "Apparently she did a lot of acting at her old school and also in summer theater."

"Big deal," mutters Josh. "She's still nothing to look at. How is the audience supposed to believe the hero falls in love with *her*?"

It's called acting, I think, but keep silent. I'm on thin ice here, and don't I know it. No one has actually said anything, but they're blaming me for Ashley's defeat, just like I said they would.

"Oh, they're just a bunch of dorks anyway," says Ashley, tossing her hair. She looks around the table, and everyone nods in agreement, which makes me feel uncomfortable, wondering if I am now one of those "dorks."

"Obviously you've got to be a member of their stupid club to get a part," says Mandy Shelton, Ashley's best friend. "It's so unfair!"

"Yeah, this Conreith guy used his influence to get his mousy girlfriend the part," says Josh. "Man, that really burns me up!"

"Simon doesn't know Deirdre; she's new to the school," I can't help reminding him and am rewarded with hostile glares.

"Yeah, well, he's probably hoping to *get* to know her," Josh says suggestively, and that gets a few half-hearted laughs. If you could see Deirdre next to Sabrina, you'd know just how funny that is.

"Ashley, why don't you try out for the spring musical?" I suggest. "They're doing *Guys and Dolls* this year — I think you'd be super in it."

"Maybe," she sniffs.

"You really should," I urge her. "You have so much musical experience. Why, you'd be a natural!"

Ashley shrugs and puts her hand on Josh's arm. "Let's get out of here," she says, pouting. "I'm not hungry, and the smell of this stuff is making me nauseous."

As if on command everyone gulps down the rest of their pizza and slurps down their Cokes. Everyone but Brian. He puts his hand over mine.

"You guys go ahead," he tells them. "Marie and I are gonna hang for a minute."

The three of them shuffle out, Josh and Mandy still telling Ashley how lousy my play is going to be without her (Thanks very much, friends) and how fab she'd be in a musical.

"What's up?" I ask Brian. "You know I can't be late for Mr. Bowman's class. His only joy in life is handing out detentions."

"Why did you stick up for that jerk?"

"I didn't stick up for him," I protest. I know exactly who *that jerk* is, of course. "I just said that he doesn't know Deirdre. Or at least he didn't before the audition."

"Boy, does that stink," he mutters.

"I know," I agree, sighing. "But what could I do?"

"For starters, you could tell them that either Ashley gets the role or you're taking your play back, that's what you could do."

"I couldn't do that! Even if I wanted to, so much work has already gone into this — " I catch Brian's scowl and take a deep breath. There are times when a little honesty is needed. "Listen, Brian," I say, looking squarely into his gorgeous face. "I'm sorry Ashley's disappointed, really I am, but the truth is, she wasn't very good."

61

"Yeah, well, she could have improved."

I let that one go. I said a *little* honesty, not a whole truckload. If Ashley improved ten times over, she still wouldn't be as good as Deirdre, but it wouldn't help to point that out to Brian.

"Would it have hurt them to give Ashley the part?" Brian demands. "What difference does it make, anyhow?"

"It makes a big difference. Opal is a pivotal role!"

"Pivotal?" Brian gives me this strange look. "Jeez, Marie, what's going on with you? Now you're even starting to talk like *them*."

"Okay, I'm sorry," I tell him. "But Opal is very important. Having the right person in the role could make or break the play."

"I don't get you. What about loyalty to your friends? Don't you care about that? Ashley's your *friend*, Marie."

"No," I reply, trembling. I am getting a little tired of people accusing me of not caring. "She's Josh's girlfriend and the most popular girl in school. But Ashley and I are not really that close."

Brian looks astonished. "Sure you are. You spend a lot of time together."

"Yes, but we don't really talk about anything." I shake my head. "Oh, I can't explain it, Brian, but please don't be mad. I did my best, honestly I did."

I put my hand over his, and look up at him with big, pleading eyes. I've practiced this look a lot, and, if I may say so myself, I've got it down just about perfect.

Brian, of course, relents, patting my hand awkwardly. "Aw, that's okay, Marie, I know it wasn't your fault. Come on, we'd better get back to school."

Didn't I tell you that looking like Snow White has its advantages?

Brian throws some money on the table and puts his arm around me as we walk out the door. His arm feels strong and safe. I lean my cheek into his sweater, liking the scratchy feel of it against my skin.

Good work, Valpacchio, I tell myself. Once again you've managed to avoid arguing with Brian. If only Simon were as easy. . . .

"Want to go to the mall with me after school?" Brian asks when we're in his car. "I need some help picking out a birthday gift for my mom."

"Oh, darn, I wish I could, but I've got rehearsals," I tell him, as if having to go to rehearsals was some gross chore like having to scrub toilets. "And after that I've got to put some time in at the library. Ugh." I smile and hope he'll smile back.

He does.

"No big deal," he says, shrugging. "We'll go another time."

But he doesn't say anything the rest of the way.

If it weren't for the fact that Simon would be there, I'd actually be very excited about the first day of rehearsals. As it is, I enter the auditorium feeling like one of those Christians thrown into the lion's den.

Mr. Phillips is not around. True to his word, he's leaving it all to us and plans only to make occasional visits to see how it's going and to "advise" us.

Simon looks surprised to see me. He probably thinks that after that tirade he handed me I'd be home with my tail between my legs.

"You don't have to be here," he tells me in his superior way. "We're only doing read-throughs today. I'm sure you have more important things to do."

"You might need me," I say stiffly.

"I doubt it."

"Well, anyway, I'd like to hear them read the dialogue. We might find other parts that need work."

Simon lifts that stupid eyebrow of his and shrugs in a way that says he couldn't care less. "Suit yourself."

I sit down next to Beverly Safare, who has been really friendly to me ever since the reading at Simon's house. She's the assistant director. Translated that means "gofer" — the one who gets all the un-fun jobs. It figures Simon would get a girl for that position.

"Okay, people," Simon yells, clapping his hands. "Settle down and get a seat down here by the stage."

He waits until everyone is sitting, a lot of them on top of the stage, before he begins again. First he introduces himself and has everybody else tell their name and what they're doing with the play. I'm last and sort of mumble my piece, but Max, who is playing Claude, Holden's uncle, yells, "Author! Author!" and claps. Simon just shoots him a look before continuing.

"Before we begin, let's get a few things straight. First off, all of you had better realize that your Monday, Tuesday, and Thursday afternoons for the next six weeks are committed to this play." He holds up a copy. "You're going to read these lines over and over again until you know them backwards and forwards — not just your own, but everyone else's, too. You're going to work, work, work, until you ask yourself why you ever wanted to be in this production. Because, in spite of what you may think, drama isn't all fun and games. It's work, discipline, dedication, and then more work."

It's a wonder he didn't add "Marie" to that last sentence. Obviously this whole spiel is directed at me.

"There are some rules we go by," Simon continues. "First, no coming in late. Second, no more than three absences, except in emergencies, or you're out. Third, no disrupting the other actors on stage. If you're not reading your scene, then find something useful — and quiet — to do. If any of you has a problem with what I just said, then I suggest you get out now and save us both a lot of time and trouble."

Simon looks around the room, pointedly ignoring me. As a pep talk, his speech isn't very good; as a welcoming speech, it's even worse. I don't even think it's original — I'm willing to bet almost anything that he got it out of some movie. You know, the hardball director and the worn-out crew, giving their all for Broadway, like in *42nd Street.*

So I'm not the only one who watches those old movies!

Simon waits, as if he's really expecting someone to get up and walk out. "Fine," he says. "We've got a lot of work ahead of us; let's get to it."

"Yes, sir!" pipes up Max. "Whatever the Supreme Commander wishes, sir!"

Everyone laughs at that — even Simon manages to smile without cracking his face. "Act one, scene one," he growls good-naturedly, and they begin.

Hearing my play read by actors is still a new experience for me. It'd be really enjoyable if Simon weren't making such a point of ignoring me, talking to Beverly between scenes like I wasn't there. It doesn't take long before I start feeling miserable and sorry for myself. How am I supposed to endure six weeks of the cold shoulder? I ask you, do I need this kind of stress?

Up on stage, Holden, his mother, and his stepfather/uncle (Adam, Sabrina, and Max) are doing the scene where Holden confirms his suspicions that his uncle killed his father. It's a very pivotal scene, since it sets off a chain of events and starts Holden on his path to destruction. Simon doesn't think it gives Holden enough to go on.

Right now they're all supposed to be sitting at the breakfast table while Holden reads the newspaper.

Holden: Well, can you believe this!

Claude: What's that, son?

Holden: (hands tremble at the word "son") Well, *Uncle* Claude, I was just reading about this murder trial going on in New York.

Grace: Oh, dear, that's not the most cheerful topic for the breakfast table, is it? I pity those poor people in New York — murders seem to be an everyday occurrence in that dreadful place.

Holden: But this one has got a new twist, Mother. It seems this man killed his own brother by drowning him in a bathtub.

(Claude stops cold. His fork drops to his plate with a loud clatter.) This doesn't actually happen, of course, since the actors have to get comfortable with their lines before they start using props.

Grace: Mercy! I never heard of anything so vile! His own brother! His own flesh and blood! Tell me, dear, how did they catch him?

Sabrina really plays up the soft, Southern accent —

I can see she's going to be a great fading Southern belle.

Holden: Well, they thought he had bumped his head and drowned, but there were strange marks on his body. They let that pass until his widow came forward with new evidence.

Grace: His widow?

Holden: Hmmm. It seems this guy murdered his brother just so he could get to his wife. He'd been in love with her for years, you see, and would stop at nothing to get her.

Grace: No! Oh, how awful!

Holden: Yes, it is, isn't it? But apparently the murderer talked in his sleep. That was what clued her in. Naturally, she went to the police when she realized the truth.

Grace: Naturally! Oh, the poor, unfortunate woman.

Holden: Well, let's just hope he gets what he deserves.

Grace: Amen to that, dear. I say hanging would be too good for him. Don't you agree, Claude? (She turns towards husband.) Claude, darling? What's the matter, dear?

Claude: (Looking very nervous at this point.) Excuse me, I have to be at the office early today.

(Exit Claude. Grace looks perplexed. Holden looks triumphant. He *knows*!)

But *how* does he know, I ask myself? Claude's reaction isn't much to go on — he could just be feeling guilty because he married his brother's widow. That's a gross enough reason to look guilt stricken — his

67

reaction doesn't necessarily prove he murdered his brother.

Although it kills me (speaking of murder) to admit it, Simon is right. Holden needs to have more proof that his father, an excellent swimmer, didn't drown in a boating accident. He needs to know for sure that his uncle had a hand in it. But how?

I look over to Simon, who is intently listening to Holden confide his suspicions to the family butler. Simon looks pretty pleased so far. Suddenly I'm not.

After rehearsals, I call my mom at work and tell her I won't be home for dinner. I go directly to the library and bury myself behind a mountain of books. That's where Tina finds me a few hours later.

"What are *you* doing here?" she asks, as if I never go to the library. Okay, the librarians don't exactly know me by name, but I do at least keep my card up to date.

"What does it look like I'm doing? I'm enriching my mind."

"That's a switch. Good God, are you really planning to read all these? *Freud and Modern Psychology, Understanding the Human Mind* — since when are you taking psych? Aren't you the one who said it was all just a bunch of baloney?"

"I said that stuff you pick up in magazines and on TV is baloney. But Freud was a *real* psychologist, not one of those sensationalist talk-show hosts you like so much. He wrote about a lot more than just sex."

"That's not what I've heard. What's that you've got in your hand?"

I hold up the book I'm reading.

"*Modern Literary Criticism of Hamlet*," she reads, pointing to the open chapter. "*Hamlet and the Oedipus Complex* — what's that?"

"An Oedipus complex is when sons love their mothers and hate their fathers," I tell her.

"Sounds pretty sick to me."

"No, apparently most little boys go through that stage. It's only sick when they don't grow out of it."

"Marie, what kind of assignment is this?"

"It's not an assignment. I'm just doing a little research for the play."

"I thought that was all finished."

"It is. I just want to make a few improvements."

"A few! This wouldn't by any chance have anything to do with your fight with Simon, would it?"

"Tina, it wasn't a fight, it was a one-sided bawling out, and I was on the receiving end."

Tina nods. She has this way of nodding that makes her look very wise. "He really got to you, didn't he?" she asks.

"Yeah," I admit. "The worse thing is that he was right. Ashley wasn't any good as Opal, and I knew it."

"Don't sweat it. You said a few words on behalf of a friend. The same as anyone would do."

"Simon wouldn't," I say with absolute certainty. "Face it, Tina, he was right. But he doesn't have to be so mean about it. You should have seen him today, the creep, acting so superior, treating me like I wasn't even there. He really has the lowest opinion of me, and he doesn't mind letting me know it."

69

"So forget him. Like you said, he's a creep."

"Yeah. It just bothers me to have someone thinking bad things about me, you know?"

Tina sighs. "Did anyone ever tell you that you worry too much about what people think?"

"You do, Tina. All the time."

"God, I'm so smart, I can't stand it," she says, rolling her eyes. "Well, I'll leave you to Hamlet and his complex. Can you give me a ride home?"

"Sure, no problem."

"Great. We'll talk more about it then."

"What, you mean Hamlet or about how smart you are? Gee, Tina, maybe you'd be a good match for Simon. He has a high opinion of himself, too."

Tina smiles. "Maybe I would."

What the heck does she mean by that?

I spend the next week dividing my time between rehearsals and working on my play. Simon still pretty much ignores me, although he has thawed out enough to say a few words to me — like "hello" and "good-bye."

Well, it's something.

By Friday all my work has paid off. I've figured out how Holden discovers his uncle killed his father. I look for Simon all day to give him my new version of the play, but I can't find him. I decide to wait for him out in the parking lot after school.

I'm standing by the turquoise bomb, stamping my feet and burrowing my face in my scarf when I see him. He doesn't see me; his shoulders are hunched, and he's got his hands shoved into his pockets. I think he's whistling, but I can't say for sure, because his dark head is bent against the wind.

He notices me, stops, and then walks quickly toward the bomb.

"Hi, Marie. What's up?"

I shove the script into his hands. "I want you to read this."

"I've already read it. Several thousand times."

"Not this one, you haven't," I snap. "I've been working on it every night since last week — including the weekend! I haven't done any work for my classes, not even studying for my tests, which probably means I'm going to flunk them. I barely got any sleep. The least you can do is read the stupid thing."

Simon looks taken aback for a minute. "Why don't we get in the car?" he suggests. "You look like you're frozen."

I don't argue. I *am* frozen. I must have been waiting for Simon for at least fifteen minutes.

He unlocks his door (the one on the passenger side is still broken) and lets me in. He starts up the car, turning the heat on full blast. It comes out cold at first, but then it starts blowing hot air. He reaches over and aims the vent right at me.

"Feel better?"

I nod, flexing my toes.

"First tell me what this is all about," he says. "What is this you've been working on so hard?"

I take a deep breath. "You know the part about how Holden knows his uncle killed his father — how you said it was illogical? Okay, he hears rumors, he has dreams, he mentions that newspaper article to his un-

71

cle and gets the reaction he hoped for — but it's not enough."

Simon nods. "Go on."

"Okay — we know that Holden's father was a big success — the town hero. Probably an authoritarian figure. Probably someone who overshadowed Holden his whole life. We also know that Holden adores his mother until she marries Claude. What if it's not just her marrying Claude that he objects to, but to her marrying anyone? What if he's just jealous?"

"An Oedipus complex. Very Freudian. Lots of critics have taken that view of Hamlet." Simon nods again. "But what's that got to do with — "

"I'm coming to that," I say, speaking quickly. "Okay, here it is. What if Holden knows his uncle killed his father because he *saw* it? He saw his uncle drown his father, and then he *blocked* it from his mind — totally erased it from his memory. Then he has dreams because he's suffering from a terrible guilt complex — because he secretly hated his father and is actually glad he's dead."

Simon looks at me, stunned. "Wow!"

"It all comes out when Claude and Holden are having the final scene — in the river," I tell him excitedly, turning to the last few pages of the script and pointing it out to him. "Holden confronts Claude, who sneers at him, because he knows Holden has this thing about his mother and he thinks it's really sick."

Simon's eyes are moving over the script quickly, intently. Then he starts reading Claude's part aloud, adding just the faintest of southern accents.

"You disgusting little twerp, you make me *sick*," he says. "Mewling around, crying about your daddy, tell-

72

ing everybody what a great man he was and how much you loved him! A bigger hypocrite never lived on God's green earth! You were glad when I killed him — don't bother to deny it. It was what you'd wanted to do for your whole life, wasn't it, Holden? But I got there first!"

"You shut up!" I say, reading Holden's lines. "Just shut your mouth. You're not going to talk to me that way!"

"I can talk to you anyway I want, sonny boy, 'cause we're two of a kind, you and me. Only I never sunk as low as you. God knows I got things to be ashamed of, but at least I'm a *man*!"

"I'm gonna kill you!"

"You? You haven't got the guts. But I do. Hell, I would have killed you a long time ago but for your mama. She justs dotes on her little boy. Now I wonder what that fine, upstanding woman would say if she knew her precious son was entertaining feelings for her that were definitely un-sonlike?"

"Shut up, you vile son of a — "

Claude starts laughing. He's still laughing while Holden pushes his head underwater and strangles him.

Simon puts the script down and looks over at me. "Wow," he repeats. "That's *good*."

"Your reading helped," I say modestly. Simon smiles and goes back to reading the script. "The ending's the same," I tell him. "Only I thought we could play a tape of Claude laughing, even though he's dead, you know, to symbolize that Holden can't run away from the truth."

"Excellent," he says, nodding his head up and down. "The whole concept — just unbelievably excellent."

I shrug. "Oh, it's no big deal. Basic psychology."

"But I can't believe you thought of it — "

"Oh, right," I say sarcastically. "What you mean is, how could a total airhead like me think of it when the intellectual heavyweight of the senior class didn't?"

Simon has the decency to look uncomfortable. "About that," he begins. "I was way out of line, over-reacting like that. I'm sorry I came down on you so hard."

His apology amazes me. I never would have thought Simon could sound so humble. Then his eyes meet mine, and another amazing thing happens. For the first time I notice that they're not brown at all — they're more like the color of honey. Shiny and kind of golden.

"That's okay," I tell him, shifting in my seat. "If you hadn't, I wouldn't have written it. You made me so angry I had to prove you wrong."

"Then maybe I'm not so sorry." He smiles. "Really, Marie, this is great. The only thing we need is a little more foreshadowing — you know, dropping little hints about what's coming in the big finale. But that won't be too hard to do. We should have it all together by next week."

"I hope the actors won't mind having to learn new lines."

"Who cares if they do? They should be grateful that they're going to be part of a history-making play."

"Get serious."

"I am serious. Come on, what do you say we go to Friendly's and celebrate? I'll treat you to the biggest ice-cream sundae you can handle."

"Ice cream? In this weather?"

74

"Make it cake, then — or pie — whatever you want. Let's splurge. Come on, you deserve it."

I laugh, suddenly feeling in the mood for ice cream — as if it were warm and sunny outside instead of freezing cold. "Sure — " I begin and stop in mid-sentence. "Oh, I can't," I say, suddenly remembering. "Brian — "

"Oh, yeah." Simon's face darkens. "I forgot about him."

So did I.

"Is he waiting for you?"

"Huh?" I glance up at Simon. "Oh, no — he's at the dentist. But still — "

"I know," Simon cuts in. "Well, I can at least drive you home. You've already missed the bus."

"Thanks," I mumble and settle back against the seat.

On the way back to my house he starts talking about the play again. We're still talking about it when he pulls up into my driveway. We sit in the car for a while, running the motor.

"Would you like to come in for um — coffee or something?" I ask after about ten minutes. It seems wasteful to be using up his gas like this.

"Coffee?" He grins. "Since when are you drinking coffee?"

"I didn't say I'd drink it — I only offered to make you some."

He shakes his head. "No, I'd better not. Thanks all the same."

Well, that's fine with me. I only offered to be polite, anyway.

He gets out and holds the door open for me. "See you Monday," he says, and I nod.

"Thanks for the lift."

"Anytime." He takes a strand of my hair and tweaks it. I usually find that really annoying, but I let it pass this time.

"Have a good weekend, Marie," he says.

"You, too," I mumble, but he's already in the car, driving away.

Six

I don't have a lot of time to think about Simon right now, because tonight Brian and I are double-dating with Tina and Mike. Yes, I finally got Brian to agree to it, and then I worked out the actual time and place with Tina. It wasn't easy. Arranging a peace summit between the major world powers probably requires less effort.

We're going out on Friday night instead of on Saturday, like Brian and I usually do, because my brothers, Paul and Jack, are home from college for the weekend. Tomorrow my parents are planning what they like to call a "family day." I, being more realistic, like to call it a "minor war." On "family days" we visit selected relatives and end up in a fight that's just short of one of the barroom brawls you see in old westerns. Nobody in my family gets along with anybody else.

Brian arrives right on time, and then we go pick up Mike and Tina. First we have trouble agreeing on a movie. Brian suggests one of those teenage slasher films, which Tina quickly vetoes. Mike suggests the new Schwarzenegger movie, which Brian has already seen. Finally we all agree on some stupid, boring comedy that nobody really wants to see, and nobody is happy.

Not the greatest beginning.

Afterwards we go to the Pizza Hut and can't agree on the kind of pizza we want. Mike and Tina want the thick crust, while Brian likes the thin kind. (I'm willing to go either way.) Mike likes anchovies; Brian doesn't, but likes onions; Tina hates onions. By this time I've lost my appetite. Finally we order two separate pizzas.

I wish we'd just gone for burgers.

The guys aren't talking very much, so it's up to Tina and me to carry on the conversation. We're trying our best to be witty and charming and are fast losing ground, when I notice a flash of red-gold out of the corner of my eye. I peer over Brian's shoulder to get a better look.

"Well, look at that," I exclaim. "Sabrina Solowick and Adam Cooke. Together! Over there, by the salad bar."

Everyone looks over. "Are they dating?" asks Tina.

"I guess so," I tell her, thinking of Simon. Does he know, I wonder? More importantly, would he care?

"They're both in the play," Tina explains to Mike. "That's where they must have met, right, Marie? God, it's so romantic, I can't stand it. It must be true love. I never thought I'd see Sabrina at a Pizza Hut."

Mike grins. "Why not? She has to eat, too, doesn't she?"

"Naturally, but pizza?"

"She's pretty," says Brian, giving Sabrina the once-over. "But her clothes are too strange."

At this point Sabrina and Adam get up to leave. They must have felt our eyes trained on their backs, because they turn toward us. Sabrina's face breaks into a smile when she notices me, and she drags Adam over.

"Hi, Marie. We were just talking about you! Weren't we, Adam?"

Adam nods dumbly, glancing at Sabrina with just the teeniest bit of awe.

"Simon called me this afternoon about what you've done with Holden," Sabrina adds enthusiastically, barely giving me time to do the introductions. "He even read me a little over the phone. I love it! Imagine seeing your father die and shutting it completely from your mind! It's so inspired! Right, Adam?"

"Oh, definitely," Adam says, his voice cracking a little on the last syllable. "I only hope I can get all the lines in time."

"Don't worry, you're going to be magnificent," Sabrina tells him. "I'll work with you if you want, day and night, if necessary. You're going to give an inspired performance as Holden, Adam, really you are."

Adam does not look convinced; he looks like a man being led to the guillotine. He must really be regretting trying out for Holden. The expression on his face as he opens the door for Sabrina is one of absolute terror. Honestly, I think he's *sweating*, and it's the middle of January, for Pete's sake. Apparently the romantic possibilities of Sabrina's promise of "day and night, if necessary," haven't hit the poor boy yet. Or maybe they have. Who knows?

"What was she talking about?" Brian asks, and I shrug.

"Nothing. Just something about the play."

" 'Just something' is only what she's been working on nonstop in the library for the last week and a half," Tina tells him.

"I thought you were doing your homework in the library," says Brian.

"Wait a minute," Mike snaps his fingers. "This is about what Tina was telling me — how your hero has got this complex about his mother, right? I had to read *Oedipus* for English class last semester. Man, that's pretty weird stuff."

"Jeez, everyone knows but me?" Brian complains.

"It's really not that interesting," I tell him. "And it's complicated."

"Well, golly whiz, teacher, maybe if you speak real slow I can understand," he says sarcastically.

So I take a deep breath and start to explain it to him. I'm only halfway into the explanation when I notice Brian's eyes starting to glaze over. I try to hurry up, but Mike keeps asking questions. Meanwhile Brian's eyes are flitting around the room, an obvious sign that he is tuning out. Suddenly he lets out a yell.

"Hey, Bergman! Over here!"

Standing in the doorway are Josh, Ashley, Mandy, and her (sometimes) boyfriend Steve. They come over to join us, crowding into our booth, with lots of kidding and wisecracking that somehow doesn't include Mike and Tina. Brian calls the waitress over to order another pizza. I exchange a look with Tina. Our double date is not turning out the way I'd planned it.

But at least Brian seems happy.

"That was fun, wasn't it?" I ask brightly after we've dropped Mike and Tina off. "Let's do it again sometime."

Brian doesn't answer right away, but I'm hoping that's because the roads are kind of icy and he's concentrating on his driving. "I don't know," he says finally. "We didn't have a lot to talk about. It's a good thing the gang came along when they did."

"Oh, sure," I lie. "Still, it's nice to go out with other people once in a while."

"But we don't have anything in common with them. I don't see why you suddenly want to hang with Tina, anyway. She's okay-looking, I guess, or she could be if she'd fix herself up some. But like, what do you have in common?"

"I don't think you should make friends based on what they look like," I tell him, the words "superficial," "shallow" — Simon's words — racing through my mind.

I think of all the things Tina and I have been through together. I remember how she was willing to listen for hours when I talked about some boy I had a crush on — sometimes there was a new one every month. She even helped me with all my schemes to get the boy's attention, like walking by his house and calling him up on the phone.

I remember when Pee Wee, her pet hamster, got sick. I went with Tina to the vet, and when he told her there was nothing he could do, I cried right along with Tina. And when Pee Wee died, I helped Tina bury him in the backyard. I even said a few words over the grave. A lot of people might think it's pretty stupid and immature for two girls in junior high to have a funeral for a rodent, but I knew how important Pee Wee was to Tina.

But what I really remember — and this is so trivial, I know — is that we have the same favorite movie, *Home From the Hill*. If you've never heard of it, don't feel bad; that probably means you have better taste than we do. It's a corny old movie, but it's really romantic and sad, and we've both seen it about a zillion times. I taped it on our VCR, and marked *Do Not Erase* all over it, so we can watch it whenever we want to. Which is often, even these days, when we don't get together as much as we used to.

I don't tell Brian any of this. "We've been friends since the seventh grade," I tell him instead, and hope that he understands.

"Sure, but what do you do together now?"

"We're not like you and Josh, Brian," I say carefully. "I mean, we don't have to *do* things — mostly we just talk. About nothing, everything, you know."

"But she's a band person. You're not. It's like those kids in the drama group. Why you want to spend so much time with them is beyond me. You're not one of them."

"Does the world have to be divided between 'them' and 'us'?" I ask. "We're all the same age, we live in the same town, we go to the same school. We have a lot of the same classes, maybe the same dreams, the same problems. We're basically all in the same boat. Don't you think that's a lot in common?"

Brian gives me this strange look, like I've suddenly turned into someone he doesn't know. Luckily, we don't have time to talk about it anymore. We're in front of my house, and I've only got a few minutes until curfew.

I don't get to talk to Tina until Sunday afternoon. She doesn't think we should try to double-date again, either.

"Let's face it, the four of us just didn't click," she says. "It's not a tragedy, Marie."

"Yeah, I know," I agree. "But let's try to get together more — just you and me, okay?"

"Definitely — when you have more time. You've been kind of tied up with the Thespians lately, you know."

"Don't *you* start," I warn.

"What, has Brian been giving you a hard time about all that rehearsing?"

"Well, not exactly a hard time," I reply. "But he's not too thrilled about the whole thing, either. He never really was, you know."

"You didn't have an argument, did you?" I hear her laugh through the receiver. "That was a stupid question, wasn't it? You never argue with anyone."

" 'Blessed are the peacemakers,' " I quote smugly.

"Except me, sometimes," she adds thoughtfully. "And Simon. Do you think that means something?"

"What are you babbling about, Tina?"

"I'm just thinking that you may be outgrowing Brian. You're changing, expanding your horizons, but your relationship is stagnating. You've found this talented person inside you, and Brian's jealous — "

"Have you been watching Oprah Winfrey again?" I ask suspiciously.

"Make jokes if you want. I still say it's significant."

"Thank you, Ms. Freud. It just so happens I'm very happy with Brian and with things just the way they are."

"So how come you're always talking about Simon?"

"I am not! You're the one who brought him up!"

"Today, maybe, but usually *you* do. You're always complaining about him. That could be significant, too."

"Tina, get serious. Okay, I admit, he's not as bad as I once thought, but — "

There's a knock on my door, and Paul sticks his head in. "Cripes, Marie, you still gabbing on the phone? Some guy's downstairs waiting to talk to you."

"Brian?" I ask, confused. Paul knows Brian, so he wouldn't call him "some guy."

"No, this one's got dark hair. Simon, I think it was?"

There's a yelp on the other end of the phone. Paul kind of rolls his eyes and starts to shut the door.

"Wait!" I yell. "Where is he waiting? Who's he talking to?" *Let it be Jack,* I pray. *Please, let it be Jack.*

Paul shrugs. "Mom or Dad. Maybe both by now." He shuts the door.

"Tina — " I say into the receiver.

"I heard!" she shouts. "Didn't I tell you it was significant? Call me later and tell me *everything*! 'Bye!"

I put down the receiver and scramble off the bed. There's no time to waste. By now Mom is probably reading Simon the riot act on the equality of the sexes, and my father is checking his clothes to make sure they're made in America by union employees.

I rush out the door and then come back. It'll only take a minute to run a comb through my hair and change into a sweater that doesn't look like I picked it up at the Goodwill. It's not like I'm making a superhuman effort to look nice, or anything like that. I'd do the same for anybody.

I find Simon in the living room with my mother, drinking, of all things, herbal tea.

"Really, Simon," my mother is saying, "when you think of how little support women have gotten in the arts, it's a miracle they — "

She stops when I enter, and Simon stands up, looking a little embarrassed. "Listen, I'm sorry to barge over like this, but I tried to reach you on the phone — "

"That was me," I tell him quickly. "Sorry you couldn't get through."

"Why should you be sorry? The thing is, I had this really great idea, and I wanted to run it by you — "

"Kathleen!" my father roars from the kitchen. "I can't find the garlic press! How am I supposed to make garlic bread without a garlic press?"

Mom smiles at Simon. "Excuse me, I think I'm needed elsewhere." And then before I can signal to her not to, she's saying, "Why don't you stay for dinner, Simon? You like spaghetti, don't you?"

Simon looks at his watch. No wonder, it's only three o'clock. He must think we are one really weird family.

"We're eating early because the boys have to go back to school tonight," Mom explains. "We don't like them driving back too late," she adds, as if her sweet little boys never, ever stayed out past eleven o'clock. Boy, have they got her snowed!

"Thanks, Mrs. Valpacchio" — Simon gives me a quick glance — "but this looks like a family thing, and I wouldn't want — "

"Kathleen!" my father roars again, ruining all of Simon's polite excuses.

"Nonsense, you're not at all in the way," Mom says, smiling. "That's settled, then." She rushes into the kitchen, just as if Simon actually agreed to have dinner with us.

When she's gone, Simon and I just sort of smile stupidly at each other and sit down on opposite sides of the couch.

"I hope I didn't interrupt — "

"I'm sorry about — " I say at the exact same time. We both shut up and smile again. Simon motions for me to speak.

"I was just going to say that I hope you like Italian food," I tell him, which is a lie. But why should I apologize to him, just because my mother invited him to dinner?

"I love it," he replies. "I just hope I didn't ruin some kind of family reunion — you probably don't get to see your brothers very often."

"Don't I wish," I groan. "The twins come home at least once a month. Otherwise they'd have to do their own laundry."

"What are you doing?" yells my father from the kitchen. "You don't put paprika on garlic bread! Wait! You're not planning to use those mushy, tasteless tomatoes in the salad, are you? I know we've got some plum tomatoes around here someplace!"

86

"Then you find them!" my mother shrieks back. I smile weakly at Simon.

"Sorry about that." Now I remember why I wanted to apologize — *because* my mother has invited him to dinner. "It's a little hectic around here now."

"Hey, I think it's great your father cooks."

"He has to," I tell him. "My mother's idea of a home-cooked meal is the drive-through at the Colonel's. Or, if she's feeling really energetic, she'll pick up Chinese. I have a theory that since cooking has always been looked upon as 'woman's work,' she feels she has to refuse to do it on principle."

"Well, I guess she's got a point."

"You wouldn't say that if you had to live on take-out food five nights a week," I say with feeling. "So, what was so important that you had to come all the way over here?"

Simon makes this funny little movement with his shoulders, kind of like a shrug, but not quite. "Well, it's not that important," he says, "but I had this idea for the beginning of the play, and I wanted to get your opinion."

Wonder of wonders. First Simon, the guy who will not be fazed by anything, is sitting on my couch, looking embarrassed. Second, Simon, the guy who has all the answers, wants *my* opinion.

"Go ahead," I urge him, leaning forward. I don't want to miss any of this.

"Right. You know where Holden wakes up screaming from a nightmare? I think we need to show what he's dreaming about."

"Fine, but how?"

"Like this." Simon starts gesturing with his hands. I notice he does that a lot when he's talking about the play. "The stage is pitch-black. We spotlight Holden, tossing and turning in bed. Then the spotlight moves to Holden's father. He tells Holden he's been murdered, and that it's up to him to punish the murderer. And then the spotlight moves to his mother and uncle, telling Holden they're planning to get married. And then the spotlight moves to a group of men from the town. You know how Holden tells the family butler that he overheard some townspeople talking about how suspicious it was that his father drowned when he was such a good swimmer, and how his Uncle Claude always did envy his brother? This way we can put their conversation on stage and skip all the third-person narrative. Really milk the drama out of the scene. Get it?"

I only have time to sort of nod before Simon continues. "Then the spotlight finally moves to Holden, who wakes up screaming. Now, if that doesn't grab the audience, nothing will."

"But won't that mean we need more actors?"

Simon shakes his head. "That's not necessary. It's only for the opening scene. We'll just use a few of the actors who have smaller parts later on."

"I like it, I really do — I mean, it makes for a bigger impact, doesn't it?" I tell him honestly. "But we're already into the second week of rehearsals. Do we have time? Won't the actors have a fit when they have to learn even more lines?"

"Don't worry so much about the actors," he says brutally. "Don't you know that actors should be treated like cattle?"

88

I pause, thinking for a minute. "Wait a minute!" I exclaim. "Alfred Hitchcock said that!"

"Hey!" Simon's face brightens. "You like Hitchcock?"

"Are you kidding? I saw *The Birds* about twenty times. Seagulls still give me the creeps — especially when I see them in groups, you know?"

"That was a good one," he agrees. "What about *Psycho*? Remember the knife in the shower scene, and the blood going down the drain? Man, that guy really knew how to scare people, and in black and white, too!"

"Don't remind me," I shudder. "I wouldn't take a shower for about a month after I saw that movie. The best part was in the end, where you find the guy dressed up like his mother, and then, in that weird, high voice — " I look over at Simon.

"Nor-man!" We chorus in unison, and then start to laugh.

Then my mother walks in to tell us dinner is ready. Simon asks her where the bathroom is, and while he's gone, I pull her aside.

"Please, Mom, no arguing tonight, okay?"

"Marie, I don't know how many times I have to tell you. We don't argue, we discuss."

"Well, could you please not discuss so loudly tonight? Just for me? This boy has a *normal* family."

"Well, you poor, underprivileged darling," she says. "I promise we'll be on our best behavior. I'm sure your father and I wouldn't want to *embarrass* any of our children."

The way she says it, I'm sure that's exactly what she's going to do. But it turns out I've misjudged her.

For once she and Dad are acting like any normal mom and dad, asking Simon the normal, nosy questions: where he lives, what his parents do, and what he's going to do when he gets out of high school come June.

That gets us safely through dinner — almost — until Simon turns to Paul and innocently asks him how he likes the University of Pennsylvania.

"I'm at Wharton — the business school," Paul tells him happily. "Starting salaries for Wharton grads are only slightly lower than those for grads from Harvard, you know. I'm looking at 60,000 easily, once I get my MBA. Then it's a condo in Aspen and my very own BMW."

"It's a sad commentary on the state of our society," says my father, "when a young man has no more on his mind than how soon after college he can buy a fancy *foreign* car. Today's youth has no concern for the less fortunate, the politically oppressed. Their value system is completely warped, they're so wrapped up in material possessions."

"Oh, Dad, get off it," Paul says lightly, looking around our tastefully decorated dining room. "You guys live pretty well. You don't work for the union out of the goodness of your heart."

"Which you should be grateful for," Mom interjects before Dad can explode, "considering what that school is costing us."

"Dad's right; it's disgusting," says Jack. "When you consider how much this country spends on bombs it *says* we're not even planning to use, when we could be spending that money on useful social programs, such as education — "

"Exactly, son," Dad nods proudly.

"By the time we graduate there probably won't even *be* a BMW for Paul to buy," adds Jack, warming up. "Or any condos in Aspen. There won't be any world at all. We'll have blown civilization into smithereens. And yet, and yet, there are *still* some stupid, ignorant people" — Jack looks directly at Paul — "who think that we can use nuclear bombs as a deterrent to war!"

"It's worked so far!" shouts Paul, and that's when the fun begins. Five minutes later they're all screaming at the top of their lungs, and Jack looks ready to pour the spaghetti sauce over Paul's head. Meanwhile I'm nervously tearing a piece of garlic bread into shreds, while sneaking looks at Simon. To give the guy credit, he's taking it really well. He doesn't try to enter his own opinion — which proves he's got some brains — he just nods calmly from time to time as if he were used to eating dinner on a battlefield.

"Simon and I are going upstairs to work now," I announce loudly, standing up, and motioning for Simon to do the same.

"Don't you want dessert?" Mom asks. "We're having chocolate chip ice cream."

"Later," I tell her, and then we make our escape, the sounds of their *discussion* following us.

"Wow!" says Simon. "Are they always like this?"

"Sometimes it's worse."

"I notice you don't get into it much."

"Would you?" I ask glumly, heading for the stairs. "Come on, the script is in my room. We might as well go there. It's the only quiet place in the house."

Simon follows me, but when he gets to the entrance of my room, he kind of hovers there, with this *look*

91

on his face. That's when I realize that inviting him to my room might have been a mistake, and that he might be getting the wrong idea. He certainly looks like he's getting the wrong idea.

Boys!

I sit down at my desk, take out pen and paper, and glance at him in a very no-nonsense way. He gets the message.

Unfortunately the only other place to sit is on my bed, and it's kind of hard to remain no-nonsense when I see Simon next to my stuffed giraffe. I mean, it gives me a funny feeling, which I really can't describe, but which I very determinedly squash. I give the script in front of me my full concentration.

After a few minutes Simon gets up and starts moving around the room, which makes me even more uncomfortable. It's a small room, filled with lots of private junk, and here he is, *inspecting* it.

"Do you think Holden's father would say 'my son' or 'my boy'?" I ask.

" 'My son,' " says Simon, looking at my bookshelves. Thank God I remembered to put those steamy historical romances under my bed.

"*Romeo and Juliet*," he reads. "*Death of a Salesman, The Glass Menagerie* — you really do like plays, don't you?"

"Most of those were for classes," I reply, which isn't the complete truth. "Do you think it sounds too corny to say 'My son, it is your duty to avenge my death'?"

"Hmmm, how about, 'My son, I ask you as your father to avenge my death'?"

"Better," I agree. "And then he says, 'The murderer

walks free, unpunished — it is you who must be my hand of justice!' "

"I like that," says Simon, glancing at my photographs. There's the one of me and Brian at the beach, then the one of us at Homecoming, and —

"Is this you?" Simon asks, holding a picture of me and my family. I nod.

"Who else? It was taken up in Maine, about six years ago."

Simon lifts that one eyebrow and gently places the frame back on the shelf. "You were pretty even then," he murmurs, and my heart skids to a full stop.

Did I hear that right? Simon thinks I'm pretty? I look at him out of the corner of my eye. My heart is working again, beating out a crazy rhythm.

Da-dum, da-dum, da-dum.

"You'd better read this for yourself and tell me if you like it," I tell him when I'm finished writing.

He comes over to the desk, but instead of taking the piece of paper from me, he leans over my shoulder and reads it, his breath warm and soft on my cheek.

By now my heart is thumping so furiously I'm amazed Simon doesn't notice it. Really, I'm not some hysterical girl who thinks every boy she meets is making a pass at her, but I'm just about positive that Simon wants to kiss me. And knowing this is making me very nervous.

"I think 'vengeance is mine' sounds too biblical," Simon says, his voice low and husky. "How about, 'I will have my revenge' instead?"

"Oh, that is better," I agree, and then, stupidly, I turn to look at him. Only I forget how close he already is; our faces almost bump, *that*'s how close he is. And there's this kind of hungry look in his eyes, and his lips are only seconds away from mine. . . .

We both hear the phone ring, and I think I gasp — the kind of sound you make during a movie when something scary happens that you aren't expecting. But I don't answer the phone. I think I've forgotten where the darn thing is. I look around the room for it, my heart still thumping wildly — *da-dum*, *da-dum*, *da-dum*.

"Marie!" yells Jack from the bottom of the stairs. "It's Brian!"

Seven

Startled, I glance at Simon, and then the two of us are both talking at once.

"I'll type this up for tomorrow — "

"I'd better get going — "

" — and hand it in to Beverly — "

"I'll see myself out — "

" — so she can make copies for the cast."

Simon jerks his head in a nod and then he zooms down the stairs. I hear the front door close as I grab the phone.

"Hello?"

"Hey, Marie, you sound out of breath," Brian says. "What took you so long?"

"Oh — I was in the other room."

"Paul said you were in your bedroom."

"That was Jack," I say quickly.

"I never can tell them apart. How did the weekend go?"

"Oh — okay. Fine. Great."

"That bad, huh?" I hear Brian chuckling on the other end of the phone. Brian knows all about my quarrelsome family, even though I've never subjected him to a dinner with them. "Did I catch you at a bad time? What are you doing?"

"Oh, nothing," I say, kicking myself the minute the words leave my mouth. *Tell him the truth,* my brain is telling me. *Tell him Simon was here.*

"Nothing special," I tell him instead like the stupid idiot I am. "You know."

"Yeah, I know, family stuff. Listen, I just wanted to tell you that I got Saturday night all fixed up. It's you and me, plus Josh, Ashley, Mandy, and Steve — it looks like those two are on again."

"On again, off again," I say with a weak laugh. "Who can keep up with them?"

"Yeah, I'm glad we're not like that," he murmurs, and I am overwhelmed with guilt. Brian can be so sweet! I'm lucky to have him as a boyfriend — why am I taking a chance on screwing it up?

"Listen, bowling okay with you?" Brian asks. "We haven't done that for months."

"Oh, sure," I tell him. Forget that my bowling average is about a fifty-seven. This is no time to quibble. "Whatever you want."

"Great!"

Brian keeps talking, but to tell you the truth I'm not really listening, just mumbling "uh-huh" and "uh-uh" at the appropriate places. What I'm really doing is thinking. Very hard. I'm thinking that I should tell

96

Brian that Simon was here — on business, of course. I should tell him, because there's always a chance he'll find out anyway. And after all, it isn't as if I've done anything wrong.

So why don't I tell Brian the truth?

Simon gives everybody the new scenes at rehearsals on Monday. There's some groaning about the extra work, of course.

"What is it with this river?" asks Adam plaintively. "First Holden's father drowns in the river, then Opal offs herself in the river, and then Claude gets nailed in the river."

"You'd think the people in that town would get the message, and have that river filled in," comments Max.

"It's symbolic," I tell them. "It's the dark and violent river running underneath the clean and sparkling world of Culpeper County."

For a second everyone stares at me. They look impressed. Especially Simon.

"So the river exposes the seamy side of small-town life, the hypocrisy of the townspeoples' values," says Sabrina, and I nod, trying to look wise and intellectual.

"Something like that," I tell her.

There's silence again, and then Max shouts, "Aw, you got that out of a book!"

I shrug, as if I couldn't care less what Max thinks. Actually, I got the idea from a movie, but no way am I going to admit it.

"It's still very profound," says Beverly loyally. "Maybe we should put something about the symbolism of the river in the program."

"We don't have time to discuss that now," Simon

cuts in. "Right now we need to read the new scenes through." But he gives me a smile to let me know he's not really annoyed. It's a private smile, aimed only at me, and for some reason it throws me into a confused panic. I look down and concentrate on turning the pages of the script.

The next day Beverly gives all the actors a roll of masking tape and a magic marker, a different color for each person. Then in each of the scenes where the actors have to move, Simon tells them exactly how many steps to take, where to turn, stuff like that. When he has them where he wants them, he yells "Stop!" Then the actors have to mark the floor with their specially colored tape.

This is what they call blocking, and it's very important. You wouldn't believe how often the actors bump into each other or stand in front of another actor, cutting them off from the audience's view.

On Thursday Beverly and I are sitting in our usual seats, waiting for rehearsal to begin. Today they're doing more blocking, which is getting real old, real fast, as far as I'm concerned. Beverly's just as bored by it as I am. She starts talking about the material that we're going to use to simulate the river.

"Want to come along tomorrow to pick it up?" she asks me.

"Where?"

"Someplace way out in Howard County. They had the cheapest price. But I told Simon I refuse to drive all that way by myself."

"Sure, okay," I agree, just as Simon appears. I give him a quick nod, then glance down. The truth is, I've been more or less avoiding Simon all week, but he's been so busy with the blocking that I don't think he's noticed.

"Hey, Boss!" Beverly greets him warmly. "Guess what? Marie's going to come with us on Friday."

I'm so surprised, I think my mouth falls open. Beverly never mentioned anything about Simon going with her before!

"Good," says Simon, giving me what they call in novels an "enigmatic look." That means I haven't the slightest idea whether he really thinks that's good or not.

"I'll drive," he says. "Meet me at my car." Then he turns away and starts bellowing at the actors to get in position.

On Friday I'm walking toward the parking lot to meet Simon and Beverly, only I see Beverly walking in the opposite direction with some guy.

"Hey, Bev!"

She turns around and looks at me like I'm the last person she's expecting or wanting to see. Then she says something to the guy next to her, whom I now recognize as Pete, who plays Luke, Holden's best friend in the play.

She walks toward me, I walk toward her — we meet somewhere in the middle.

"Did you forget?" I ask her. "Today's the day we're supposed to get the material."

She shakes her head and clutches my arm. "Please, please, please, don't tell Simon you saw me with Pete! I told him I had to pick up my little sister for my mother. I had to lie, Marie! Simon doesn't understand why anyone wants any life outside of the play. That's all he thinks about! Say you don't hate me for skipping out on you like this."

"But, Bev — "

"Please, please, please, don't be mad. I've had a crush on Pete for the longest time — finally he asks me out for a soda — it's not my dream date, but it is a beginning. I had to say yes!"

"I understand, Bev, but — "

"I knew you would! You'd do the same, wouldn't you — that is, if you didn't already have a boyfriend."

That's right, I do have a boyfriend, I think. One who isn't thrilled about me going somewhere with Simon and Beverly in the car. But when he hears that it's just me and Simon — alone — he's going to have a fit.

"Why don't you and Pete come with us?" I suggest.

Beverly looks at me like I've escaped from a mental institution. I guess I deserve that.

"Never mind," I mumble. "Go ahead. You had to pick up your sister for your mother; Simon won't hear different from me."

"Thanks," Bev says gratefully, squeezing my arm. "You're a true friend, Marie."

A true wimp is more like it, I think, hitching up my books as I approach the turquoise bomb. Now I'm going to be stuck with Simon — alone — for at least two hours.

I look up at the darkening sky and then burrow my chin into my scarf against the wind. It's turning bitterly cold again.

Simon is waiting for me in the car. As soon as I get inside, he hands me a map. "I'll drive," he says. "You navigate."

So of course we get lost. But only a little bit. We take the wrong exit, and Simon has to backtrack a few miles.

"Sorry," I say. "I have no sense of direction."

"Cripes, that's such a *feminine* thing to say."

Now if Brian were to say that, he'd be teasing, and he'd make the being feminine part sound like a compliment. Simon isn't teasing; he's *sneering*, and he makes calling someone feminine sound like the worst insult possible.

"Sorry," I say again, before I can stop myself.

"Stop apologizing, will you? You don't have to act so nice all the time."

"It isn't an act," I tell him coldly. "I am nice."

"Okay, be nice. But don't put on that dumb-sweet-little-thing act with me. You're too smart to act stupid."

"I never said I was stupid; I said I have a lousy sense of direction. Einstein couldn't even remember his own address, and he was a genius! Anyway, since when did you start thinking I was smart? I thought I was an airhead."

Simon groans. "You're never going to let me forget that one, are you? I said I was sorry, if you remember. Besides, you've probably said a lot worse things about me."

He gives me a quick glance when I don't reply. What can I say? I have said a lot worse things about Simon — and they're not half as bad as some of the things I've *thought* about him. But at least I've never said anything to his face.

"Haven't you?" Simon prods.

"This is so stupid," I tell him. "What are we arguing

about? Let's just drop it, okay? I hate to argue."

"I've noticed. That's one of your biggest problems. You always run away at the first sign of a fight."

"And you always run toward it!" I say angrily. I'm doing my best to stay reasonable, but he is really pushing me. "Why are you being so hostile?" I demand.

"I don't know what you mean," he says, his voice very cool and even. He shoots me a quick glance, and right away I realize that Simon *has* noticed that I've been avoiding him all week. And he is obviously ticked off about it. Honestly, and I thought I was doing us both a favor!

Several minutes pass by in silence, while I'm thinking about what I can say to him to make it all right. Then we're pulling into a huge parking lot, and it's too late. Best to let it drop, I think.

The fabric store is a big warehouse out in the middle of nowhere. I mean, *nowhere.*

"Oh, you're here for the thirty-six yards of blue faux-silk?" the clerk asks us.

We nod.

"That's an awful lot of material," she says, leading us to the back. "Are you planning to make your own bridesmaids' gowns, hon?"

It takes a minute for her question to sink in. "No!" I exclaim, horrified. I look at Simon, who seems totally unfazed, as usual. Maybe he didn't understand what she said. Or maybe nothing ever embarrasses him like it does me.

"It's for a school play," Simon explains calmly.

"Oh, I thought she looked young," the clerk says, giving both of us the eye. "But you never know these days. We do a lot of wedding business."

I look around the huge warehouse and see that she's telling the truth. The place is full of these truly tacky mannequins dressed up in wedding gowns that don't fit right. Also, the walls are covered with posters of brides and bridesmaids.

"What's faux-silk?" I ask her.

"One hundred percent polyester, but with the look and feel of real silk," she says, holding out the material for me.

I touch it. "Maybe to the audience it will look like silk," I say dubiously.

"It's supposed to look like water," Simon reminds me, brushing my hand as he reaches for the material. "But the color is right. It'll do."

Simon pays for the material, and we walk out of the store. Outside it's sleeting so hard and so fast that we can barely see the car.

"Oh, great," says Simon. "That's all we need. On top of all the snow we've been having — the roads are going to be pure ice."

I look up at the nearly pitch-black sky. "Maybe we should wait it out?"

"How long do you have? Two, three days?" He frowns. "No, we'd better start heading home now."

We get into the bomb, and Simon immediately turns on the headlights and shuts off the radio. "I can't concentrate with that on," he tells me. "Mind?"

I shake my head, staring out the window at the snow piled up high against the side of the road. "No, I'll be quiet."

"You don't have to be quiet. Go on, talk to me."

From Simon this simple request comes out like a command, but I know he's trying — *so* hard for him —

to be civil. Apparently the foul mood he was in has passed. I search around in my head for something to say.

"Rehearsals are going really well," I tell him, falling back on familiar ground. "A lot better than the weather," I joke halfheartedly.

"They're getting there," Simon agrees. "We'll probably have to call extra rehearsals toward the end, though."

"Adam has really been working hard. It shows, don't you think? When he's with Sabrina — wow! You were right about those two," I tell him grudgingly. "They act great together."

"With them I think it's more than just acting," he says, smiling. "It happens every play. So far we've got Sabrina and Adam, Max and Deirdre — " He glances at me sideways. "Who do you think is next?"

I stop myself just in time from mentioning Bev's burgeoning romance with Pete. "I didn't know about Max and Deirdre," I tell him instead. "It's all kind of incestuous, isn't it? I mean, Adam's dating Sabrina, who plays his mother in the play. And Deirdre with Max — that's the uncle of the guy she loves."

Simon laughs, and as great as his smile is, his laugh is a hundred times better. "Yeah, you've got a point," he says. "But I'm glad Sabrina's hooked herself up with Adam. She was dating some older college guy last semester. She was pretty depressed when it fizzled out."

"It doesn't bother you?"

"What?"

"Oh — " I feel myself blushing. "I guess I thought you and Sabrina . . ." I let the question hang. He picks it up.

"No — we've just been friends for a long time," Simon replies. "I'm not like you. I don't think it's a good idea to be tied down at our age. I've got college next year, you know."

"What col — "

"How — " he begins at the same time.

"You first," he says.

"No, you — " I insist.

Simon clears his throat. "It wasn't important. I guess you and the jock have been going together for a long time, right?"

"Since last August."

Simon looks at me. "Is it serious?"

I shrug. "That depends."

"Depends how?"

"On what you call serious," I tell him, wondering why I just don't tell him to mind his own business. "We're not planning on getting married or anything like that, if that's what you mean."

"What I mean is, do you go out with other — damn!" Suddenly his eyes snap forward and his hands clench the steering wheel.

And then the car is spinning around and around, totally out of control. I see the tree in front of us and scream. We're going to crash right into it!

I put my hands over my eyes. I hear the screech of brakes and look through my fingers. We missed the tree. Now the front of the car is heading for a snowbank!

Simon's arm shoots out in front of me just before we tunnel into the snow. Then there's this loud *uumph* sound and I'm jerked back against the seat. My head bumps painfully against the doorframe.

Then everything is still.

"Are you all right?" I hear a voice ask in the darkness. I just sort of stare dazedly at the windshield, waiting to get my breath back. It happened so fast, and now it's all over.

The inside light comes on.

"Marie?" Simon's voice is sharp with concern. "Are you hurt?"

"I — I don't think so." Carefully I touch my head. It smarts.

"Here, let me see." He leans over and takes my face gently in his hands. "It's only a bump," he says. "Damn! We were on the ice before I knew it! I didn't even see it coming!"

"It's not your fault," I say, because I can tell he feels bad about losing control of his car. Guys can be very touchy about things like that.

"It's a good thing there weren't any other cars around," he mutters. "Are you sure you're all right?"

I nod, looking up into his face. "You're bleeding!"

"Yeah, my chin hit the steering wheel." He rubs at it, but there's still some blood left. I fumble in my purse for a Kleenex and start dabbing at it. The cut doesn't look too deep.

"I don't think you'll need stitches," I say. "Does it hurt?"

"Not too bad." He grins. "It feels sort of like somebody slugged me."

It occurs to me that if Simon hadn't thrown out his arm like that to protect me from hitting the dashboard, he might not have been hurt at all. I feel a rush of gratitude toward him and try to smile back. Only I'm shaking too hard.

"What do we do now?" I ask. Even to my own ears I sound scared.

"Hey, it's okay," Simon says, patting my shoulder. "We'll get out of here. No problem."

"I know, I know." I tell him, taking a deep breath. "I'm all right, really. I guess I'm just feeling kind of shaky."

I half expect Simon to tell me how *feminine* I'm being, but all he says is, "We're lucky. It could have been worse."

I nod, shivering. We *are* lucky. Very, very lucky. I start shivering even more.

Simon keeps patting my shoulder, only it feels different now, more like the way you would pet a cat. Long, soft strokes — very soothing. I look up at him, then down to my lap when I realize how close we are. His hand is closed over mine. Suddenly I don't feel so comfortable anymore. I feel a little nervous. Not a bad kind of nervous, but the kind of nervous you feel when you're not sure what you're getting into.

I try to edge away.

"You stay in the car," he tells me quietly. "I have a shovel and some salt in the trunk. Don't worry, I'll have us out of here in no time."

I cross my arms over my chest and watch Simon get the shovel and start to dig us out. The snow is really high, and he's working very hard. Even though he's not as athletic as Brian, he must have some muscles. It's hard to tell underneath his ski jacket, though.

I feel useless, like the helpless female I sometimes pretend to be. I unbuckle my seatbelt and open the door.

"What are you doing?" he asks. "I thought I told you to wait inside."

"I want to help."

"I only have one shovel."

"There must be something I can do," I tell him, bracing myself against a strong gust of wind. The sleet has turned to snow, and it is really flying; I can feel my hair getting matted where my hood doesn't cover it.

"Well, if you insist — get the salt out of the trunk and bring it back here."

The salt weighs a ton, but I get it, and we start sprinkling it under the tires for traction.

"The car is okay, isn't it?" I ask, worried.

"Sure it is." He flashes me a grin. "I told you they don't make them like this anymore!"

This time I smile back.

It takes us forever to dig the car out, but when we do, we let out a "Hooray!" and rush inside. Simon turns the heat on full blast. I take off my gloves and start rubbing my hands together.

"Brrr! I'm frozen," I say.

"Here, let me." He takes my hands in his and starts rubbing furiously. "It's quicker that way," he tells me.

In a minute the warmth comes back to them. Only the rest of me is feeling warm, too. I draw my hands away and try to comb through my hair with my fingers.

"God, what a mess. I'll never get all the knots out. I think we're going to have a blizzard, don't you? Over the weekend, too — just our luck. By Monday it'll be all cleared up. No snow days."

Simon doesn't answer. He's giving me that hungry look again, his eyes so shiny and golden, his dark hair falling across his forehead. He's gorgeous, I realize with a shock, and then my heart starts thudding like someone's banging on a kettle drum.

Da-dum, da-dum, da-dum.

"You'd better start the car, don't you think?" I know I'm babbling, but I can't help myself. "My parents are going to be frantic. Yours will probably be — "

He cuts me off with a kiss. No warning — he just bends his head and kisses me. I don't have time to stop him or react or anything like that. There's just enough time for my brain to register the fact that this is one great kiss before he breaks it off.

I stare at him, he stares at me, and my stomach lurches in a funny way. He leans forward to kiss me again, but this time I duck my head. "We've got to go now," I say firmly. "It's getting late."

I don't see it, but I can feel Simon lifting that eyebrow of his. And then he starts the car.

We don't talk on the way home. The roads are super-slippery, so Simon really has to concentrate on his driving. For which I am extremely grateful. Even if we could talk, I wouldn't know what to say. I know I should be mad, but I'm not. Maybe I should be mad at myself, but I'm not. Mostly I just feel confused. And guilty.

"I'll walk you to the door," Simon says, when we pull into my driveway.

"No, don't bother."

"It's no bother. I think I should explain to your parents about the accident."

"I'll do it."

"I don't want them thinking I'm irresponsible," he persists, and there's a stubborn set to his jaw.

109

"They *won't*, Simon. Let's just drop it, okay?"

"Easy for you," he says quietly. "What are you so afraid of, Marie?"

I don't answer that. I yank open the door — thank God Simon finally had it fixed — and slam it behind me.

Both my parents are waiting for me when I open the door, and I start to explain to them what happened. The phone rings, and Mom smiles at me. "That will be Brian. He said he'd call back around this time."

I go to answer it. It's Brian.

"Where have you been?" he demands. "I saw Beverly at Friendly's with Pete Rabinowich. I thought she was supposed to be with you."

"She was," I say as calmly as I can. "But she changed her mind. I'm late getting back because we had an accident."

That stops him for a moment. "Are you okay?"

"I'm fine. We just spun on some ice and ended up in a snowbank."

"That jerk," Brian grunts. "It figures he doesn't even know how to handle a car."

"Brian, it wasn't his fault. It could've happened to anybody. Anyway, I was distracting him."

"*What?*"

"I mean, we were talking," I say quickly.

"It must have been some conversation for it to be so *distracting* that he couldn't even keep his eyes on the road. What were you talking about?"

"The play," I lie. I wait for Brian to speak, but his side is quiet. I can feel my brain working in overdrive, planning my strategy.

110

If there's one thing I've learned from dating a football player, it's that sometimes the best defense is a good offense. Trying to sound really hurt, I say, "Brian, I just can't believe this, but it sounds as if you're *accusing* me of something."

There's a pause, and then Brian says, "No, no, it's not that. But, jeez, Marie, I don't like the idea of you and that jerk going off together. How do you think that makes me look?"

It's all I can do not to say something really sarcastic to him. I mean, the way he's going on, it's like he cares more about how he looks to his buddies than that I survived a potentially fatal accident.

But of course, I keep my mouth shut. I've had enough stress for one day. And I don't need reminding that I'm not without blame. After all, the afternoon wasn't as innocent as I'm making it out to be to Brian.

When Brian comes to pick me up for our date on Saturday night, I can tell that he's still in a ticked-off mood. So much for my strategy! It doesn't help any that there are a lot of kids from Magothy High at the bowling alley, and every one of them feels compelled to come by and ask me about the play. Some of them I don't even know. But it does give some interest to an otherwise boring evening. I'm a terrible bowler.

"Come on, Marie, you're not even trying," Brian says when yet another one of my balls hits the gutter. He's right; I'm not trying. Bowling is such a boring and stupid game. It's not even good exercise, except for your right arm.

Afterwards we all go to Pizza Hut, where all the kids who weren't at the bowling alley stop by our table and

111

ask me about the play. This doesn't improve Brian's mood any, and all the way back to my house he's complaining about how much time I spend on the play, and how I'm always talking about it. That last part strikes me as very unfair. I didn't force any of those people to come by and ask me about the play, did I?

"It's only for a few more weeks," I tell Brian. "Football and baseball seasons last a lot longer."

"I don't know why you wanted to get involved in this thing," he mutters.

"Well, you have interests, why shouldn't I? You were always telling me before how I should get involved in school activities — how good it looks on college applications and all that stuff."

"I meant getting involved in something normal. Like cheerleading."

"I don't want to be a cheerleader. Not everyone does, you know."

"Ah, you were just scared," he says, which makes me realize that Brian really doesn't know me at all. There are a lot of reasons I didn't want to try out for cheerleading, but being scared wasn't one of them.

"You would have been great — and you'd look cute in one of those outfits," he continues. "Now you're hanging out with those jerks."

"They're not jerks just because they're different from you."

He gives this snort of laughter. "They're different, all right. The *guys* sure are different."

That's such a typical jock comment I almost feel sorry that Josh and Steve aren't with us to appreciate it.

112

"Not every guy has to play sports like you," I say.

"Hey, even Mike is on the track team."

"What does Mike being on the track team have to do with anything?" I try to keep my voice low, but it's a strain. I'm actually feeling angry at Brian.

He shrugs. "Ah, forget it, I don't want to argue with you. We never used to argue at all. It's just not like you to, Marie." There's this long pause, and then he looks at me from his side of the car. "You're changing," he says in a faintly accusing tone. "You used to be sweet all the time, and — "

"Dumb?" I supply, and he shakes his head.

"No, not dumb. Come on, why are you jumping down my throat all of a sudden? I just want the old Marie back. Is that so bad?"

I know if we continue to fight we'll end the evening by breaking up. Is that what I really want? Brian's eyes look so sad and troubled, and suddenly I don't feel angry anymore. I feel sad and troubled, too.

"No, it's not so bad," I tell him. "I'm sorry, Brian. But this whole thing will be over in a few weeks. Can't you try to be patient?"

"I am trying." He sighs, pushing his fingers through his blond hair in a way I've always loved. "But I'll try harder," he promises, pulling me close.

We start to kiss, but I'm not really into it tonight. My mind keeps wandering in the strangest directions. But I let the kiss go on for a few minutes before I gently pull away. I don't want to hurt Brian's feelings.

"Marie — " he says, but I'm not listening. My eye is caught by something passing down the street. I can't see it very well, but it's big and bright, and it looks an awful lot like Simon's turquoise car.

113

Eight

"And you're positive it was Simon's car?" Tina asks me the next day. We're sitting in my room, stuffing our faces with Cheez Doodles and Diet Coke. We don't even care what a disgusting combination that is, which tells you how involved we are in the conversation.

"Well, pretty positive," I answer. "That car really stands out — there couldn't be two of them that same color. Weird, huh?"

"Yeah. I thought only girls did stupid stuff like driving by the house of the boy they have a crush on. To think boys do it, too! Wow, Marie, he must really have it bad for you."

"You really think he has a crush on me?" I ask, and she gives me this Are you kidding? look.

"Are you kidding?" she asks. "What's more, you have a crush on him, too. Go on, admit it!"

"Please, Tina — I grew out of crushes a long time ago. Okay, Simon's interesting, I admit that much — "

"Oh, is that why you kissed him? Because he's *interesting*?"

"Cut it out, Tina," I say, squirming uncomfortably. "You know Brian's my boyfriend."

"Oh, excuse me," she says in this superior tone. "Is that for all eternity and I didn't hear about it? Like, is it written in stone someplace?"

"Come on, Tina, you know how it is."

"Sure." She nods, taking another Cheez Doodle. "Brian represents security. No hassles. He makes it easy for you, letting you hang out with the popular crowd without having to do anything but be his girlfriend."

"Do you have to make me sound so — " I stop myself just in time from saying "superficial." "I happen to really like Brian, you know!"

"What about Simon?" Tina asks, then laughs — probably at my expression. "Gotcha!" She squeals, pointing her finger at me. "Why won't you just admit you're bonkers about him?"

"I'm not *bonkers* about him," I deny, "but — " I search around for the right words to describe the mixed-up way I feel about Simon, but all that comes to mind is that kiss in his car. I can feel the tips of my ears go pink just thinking about it.

"Okay, okay," I tell her, "I guess I sort of like him. Satisfied?"

Tina flops across the bed and leans back on her elbows. "Only if you are."

I look down at my orange-stained fingertips. "It probably doesn't make any difference if I am or not.

He told me he doesn't want to get tied down to anyone."

"Everyone says that," Tina dismisses. "Nobody really means it."

I wonder if Tina is right. Not just about that, but about everything. After all, one kiss isn't exactly a vow of eternal love and devotion, and it is conceivable that Simon had a legitimate reason for driving by my house Saturday night. Anyway, since when did Tina become an expert in matters of the heart? I've dated more guys than she has.

But if she is right . . . my heart skips a beat just thinking about the possibilities. It's as if knowing that Simon is definitely interested in me has made me a whole lot more interested in him.

I wonder what it would be like to go on a date with him? Where would we go? What would we do? Maybe go to a foreign film, or even a play, and then out for a late-night dinner in a little out-of-the-way restaurant, the kind that puts its menu on a chalkboard. We'd eat pasta and talk about all the things we may or may not have in common until the wee hours of the morning.

Pretty soon I'm wondering about this so hard that it's almost impossible to concentrate on what Tina is saying. It's something about Mike and about the new piece she's working on for band. I force myself to listen; fair is fair. Still, as much as I like to talk to Tina, I'm glad when she finally leaves so I can get down to some serious thinking.

Only each time I try to think about how I really feel about Simon, like really focus on what's inside of me, Brian gets in the way. Face it, going out with

Simon would mean I'd have to break up with Brian first, and I'm not sure I want to do that.

First of all, what would Brian do if I broke up with him? Probably get mad, say bad things about me to his buddies, maybe even beat Simon up! Let's say Brian does take it well. It would still be really awkward, with everyone we know taking sides, and most of them siding with Brian. I don't even want to think about it.

Not that I have a whole lot of choice. Brian and Simon, Brian and Simon; the two of them run around in my head until I feel like I'm about to explode from all this tension. It's two o'clock in the morning before I finally drift off to sleep, and I still don't know what I should do.

On Tuesday Simon asks a few of the actors to stay late to work out some of the rough spots. Afterwards Max suggests we all go out to eat at some Mexican joint. It's taco Tuesday, which means the tacos are all half-price. It's lots of fun, even if the tacos are terrible. At least the conversation is good. We talk about plays, and then about old TV shows, and finally about movies. Max asks everybody their favorite movie of all time, and I lie. No way am I going to admit to *Home from the Hill*.

"Aw, all the girls like *Gone With the Wind*," says Max. "I'm disappointed, Marie. I thought our wonderful playwright would go for something more classic."

"*Gone With the Wind* is a classic!" Deirdre says.

"He means something like Olivier's *Hamlet*," says Adam. "I rented that on video. It hasn't even been colorized yet!"

117

"I've never seen it," I confess, looking around the table. "To tell you the truth, I've never seen anything by Shakespeare."

"That gives me an idea," says Beverly. "They're doing a Shakespeare play over at the University of Maryland in April. I think it's *The Merchant of Venice*. Why don't we all go together? It'll be sort of a reunion for us after our play is finished."

"Good idea," nods Sabrina. "Kathleen Turner got her start there, you know."

"Great legs on that babe," Max whistles, and Deirdre punches him in the arm.

"Sexist! What about her acting?"

"That's good, too," Max says. "But the legs don't hurt any."

All through this exchange Simon and I haven't spoken. But he's looking at me, and I know he's looking at me, and he knows that I know that he's looking — well, you get the idea.

"Do you want to go?" he asks me, and something in his voice makes my stomach do funny things that have nothing to do with the tacos. It's like he's asking for *himself*.

"Sure, it sounds like fun," I say as calmly as I can. I'm trying to look cool and nonchalant, which is pretty hard to do with taco filling dribbling down your chin. So I just sit back and stir my Coke with my straw.

"Maybe you'll write an adaptation of that one, too!" says Max, but I don't think that's likely, since I have no idea what *The Merchant of Venice* is about.

I look around the table, and suddenly I feel sad. Rehearsals will be over soon — by April the play will be a fading memory. I'm really going to miss it. The rehearsals, the people, and having something interesting and *important* to do.

I get kind of lost in thought, and I don't really notice when Sabrina and Deirdre go to the bathroom, and Max and Adam go off to play a video game. I don't notice until Simon and I are the only ones sitting at the table. Honestly, I'm not a suspicious person, but everyone leaving at the same time does seem awfully convenient. I wonder if he planned it? Not that I'm sure I'd mind if he did.

"So, were your parents mad about the other night?" Simon asks, and that gives me a start until I realize that he's talking about the accident and not about the other thing.

"No, I explained it to them. They don't blame you."

Simon nods, playing with the salt shaker, which is inches from my hand. "Did you explain it to your boyfriend, too?"

I shrug my shoulders. No way am I going to answer that one.

"Is he going to beat me up when he hears about this?"

"Why?" I ask, meeting his intense stare for the first time. "We're only talking."

For once he keeps both eyebrows in place. "Hmm-hmm," he murmurs, like he doesn't really believe it. I'm not so sure I do, either.

Simon puts down the salt shaker in a very purposeful way and opens his mouth like he's about to make an important announcement. But then Deirdre and Sabrina come back, followed by Adam and Max, and the moment is gone.

This time I start playing with the salt shaker. Simon

has to settle for the bottle of hot sauce. We sit there and toy with the condiments and don't speak to each other for the rest of the evening.

As I drive home I start thinking about ways to break up with Brian.

By the time I pull into our driveway, I still haven't figured out how, but I know it's got to be done. I can't go on like this. I'm not cut out to be a two-timing sneak. It's no use trying to tell myself I haven't actually done anything wrong; I *feel* wrong. Like a real lowlife.

Then I go inside the house, and I feel even lower than a lowlife, if that's possible. Mom greets me with the news that Brian has broken his leg and that the doctor doesn't think he's going to be able to play baseball this season.

"This is going to break his heart!" I tell Mom, and then I realize that I've been planning to do the same thing. Okay, maybe losing me wouldn't exactly break his heart the way losing a season of baseball will, but it wouldn't make him feel any better, either.

I go to see Brian at his house the next day. He's propped up in bed, staring listlessly at the TV. His face is very pale, and the smile he gives me when I enter his room is halfhearted at best.

I give him a kiss on the cheek. "How're you feeling?"

"Pretty lousy. You heard what the doctor said about no baseball?"

I nod. "I'm really sorry, Brian."

"Me, too," he agrees. "And it was so stupid! I tripped on the sidewalk while jogging! Can you believe that?"

Actually, I can. Brian is sort of accident-prone. Or

maybe it's just that he's always doing things where injuries are more likely to happen. I'd like to suggest he give up athletics altogether, but I figure he hears that enough from his mother.

I run into Mrs. Mayor down in the kitchen. I'm scooping up a bowl of the ice cream I brought for Brian — his favorite, Pralines 'n' Cream from Baskin Robbins. Not as traditional as flowers, but I knew Brian would much prefer something good to eat.

"I suppose we should be thankful," Mrs. Mayor says with a sigh. "It could have been much worse."

I don't see how — I mean, how many people die by tripping on the sidewalk?

"It's a good thing he has a girlfriend like you to help him through this," she adds, patting my shoulder. "We're depending upon you to help cheer him up. Poor boy, he's so terribly depressed! He's going to need all the love and support we can give him, Marie."

I think she's laying it on a little thick — it's not like Brian will never walk again. But then I think of Brian's pale face and start to feel petty and mean. I guess Brian really does need me now.

I start to spend every afternoon with Brian. He has other friends visiting him, of course, but he says he wants me around. So I go, taking him his school assignments and trying my best to cheer him up. This isn't easy, because he is in one lousy, grumpy mood, and Pralines 'n' Cream from Baskin Robbins isn't doing it anymore.

Spending every afternoon with Brian means I'm not spending it at rehearsals. Of course, I'm expecting Simon to get on my case about it. But I'm still a little surprised to find him waiting for me one day by my locker, his big, bushy eyebrows nearly obscuring his eyes in a scowl.

"You've missed more than three rehearsals," he says. "You know the rules."

I'm so tired I could lean my head against the locker and sleep standing up. Instead I start to fiddle with the combination. "Then fire me," I tell him. "Didn't you hear what happened to Brian?"

"What, you're his private nursemaid?"

You'd have to be blind, deaf, and dumb to miss his sarcasm. I start shoving books into my locker. "Give me a break, would you, Simon? All the rewriting is done. It's not like you need me anymore, do you?"

He doesn't answer, unless scowling can be considered an answer. A second later he turns on his heel and stalks away.

Bang! I slam my locker shut. Somehow that makes me feel a little better.

Dinner that night is Chinese take-out, and the conversation is the St. Valentine's Day Dance at Magothy High. I didn't think I'd be going this year, but Brian's doctor told him he could go as long as he doesn't move around very much.

That means no dancing, of course. That's kind of hard to avoid at a dance, but it can be done. I know boys who never miss a school dance and have yet to step out on the dance floor.

"Do those flats of yours go with your dress?" my mothers asks.

I nod, while shoveling in more lo mein. Being able

to wear flats is the one good thing about Brian not being able to dance. Usually I have to wear heels if we're going to dance or else my head ends up practically on his belly button. But now I can wear flats and be comfortable.

"They're perfect," I tell her. "I got a pair of clip-on bows to put on them."

"You can borrow my little black bag if you want," Mom offers.

"Thanks." My dress is black velvet with bright pink piping and a satin bow in the back. Mom's bag will go great with it.

"You don't seem too excited about going," Dad comments.

I shrug. "It's no big deal."

"No big deal!" Dad repeats, chuckling. "Kathleen, our little girl sure has gotten blasé all of a sudden! There was a time when all she talked about were these dances. She used to keep her corsages in the fridge for weeks afterwards, remember?"

"It's not that formal a dance, Dad."

Mom puts down her chopsticks and looks across the table at me. "Mind telling us what's the matter, Marie?"

I wonder what they would do if I told them the truth.

"Just tired, I guess."

"Well, you've been spending a great deal of time with Brian. Your loyalty is commendable, of course, and your father and I do feel for him, being so disappointed about not being able to play baseball, but — "

"We don't want you knocking yourself out," my father finishes for her. "Or neglecting your schoolwork, either."

I shake my head like I'd jump out of a plane or sell top-secret documents to the Russians before I would ever even *think* about neglecting my schoolwork, and that seems to satisfy them. They get back to the argument they were having before dinner. It's about the lack of parking downtown, if you can believe it. Parking! No one in their right mind argues about parking! Everyone knows and agrees that there isn't enough — what else is there to be said?

"Would you two cut it out?" I suddenly explode. "Do you have to argue about everything?"

"We're not arguing," Mom says. "We're — "

"Yeah, I know, *discussing*. What's the difference?"

I didn't mean that as a request for a definition, but Dad starts giving me one anyway. "Well, honey, an argument makes you feel bad. When you argue sometimes you say hurtful things, things you want to take back later but can't. A discussion, on the other hand, makes you feel good, alive. It's like exercise for your mind. I didn't marry your mother just for her looks, you know."

This is the sort of comment that usually gets a sharp retort from Mom, so I'm amazed when she just laughs and says, "And we know it wasn't for my cooking, either!"

Then they're smiling and laughing, and honestly, it's almost worse than when they argue. Luckily the phone rings.

"That's Brian," I tell them, jumping up. "I told him I'd come over tonight and study history with him."

"Don't be home too late," Dad shouts behind me.

* * *

The night of the St. Valentine's Day dance arrives. Brian and I go with Josh and Ashley. Mandy and Steve have to go in another car because Brian has to stretch his leg out, which means he takes up the whole back-seat of Josh's Pontiac.

If you've ever been to a dance where you haven't been able to dance, then you really know what it means to be *bored*. I sit with Brian and a bunch of other people and talk about how nice the decorations look and boring stuff like that. I don't even have Tina to talk to — she went with Mike to his cousin's wedding.

Steve takes pity on me and asks me to dance while Mandy's in the bathroom. We stop dancing as soon as she gets back, though; their frequent break-ups are mostly due to her intense jealousy, and I don't want to get in the middle of one of their horrendous fights. Last Homecoming they split up right on the dance floor. It was not a pretty sight, but it sure livened things up. Everybody was talking about it for weeks afterwards.

We're all sitting together, enjoying the music, and then I notice Simon, of all people, standing by the door. Unfortunately everybody else, and I mean *every-body* else, notices at the same time.

"What's that jerk doing here?" Brian snarls.

"It is a school dance, Brian," I remind him casually, like I'm not dying to know the answer to that question myself.

Brian gives me an accusing look. "I've never seen him at one before!"

Neither have I. This isn't his sort of thing at all. He's even wearing a jacket and a tie, and he looks

125

incredibly sophisticated. I stretch my neck and try to see if he brought a date. Most people bring dates to these things, but it's not mandatory, like at a prom.

But either Simon came alone or his date's in the bathroom. I say he came alone. Call it a hunch.

"Why are you staring at him?" demands Brian, and I turn away quickly. The next time I get a chance to sneak a look, Simon isn't by the door anymore. I don't see him anywhere.

I figure he came and left already, and I feel a little flat, like a balloon that's run out of air. I go get some punch for Brian.

Suddenly Simon is right next to me.

"What are you doing here?" I demand, startled, sloshing some of the punch over my hand.

He shrugs. "It is a school function. I go to this school. Would you like to dance?"

We look out to the dance floor, where couples are swaying to the beat of a really slow song. I shake my head. "Uh — no, I can't. I mean, I'm with Brian."

"He's got a broken leg. I don't." Simon gestures toward his two perfectly working legs. But what I'm looking at are his shoulders. That's where my head reaches, even in flats. So, if we were to dance slow, I could nestle my head right on his chest.

"No — " I shake my head. "Brian wouldn't like it." I glance over at Brian, who is already fuming. If he were a cartoon, smoke would be coming out of his ears. Believe me, if Brian could get over here without totally losing his cool, Simon would be dead meat.

Simon's eyes follow mine. "Yeah, he looks angry. Do you think he's going to beat me up?"

126

"You're obsessed with that," I tell him crossly, but he just shrugs again.

"He's bigger than me. Plus he's got a crutch."

"Everyone's bigger than me."

"Scares you, too, huh?"

I crack a tiny smile — I can't help it.

"Do you know you're absolutely beautiful?"

I stop smiling.

"Do you also know that I'm crazy about you, and the sight of you with all these other men makes me mad with jealousy?"

I stand there, open-mouthed.

"What's the matter?" he asks quietly. "Did you forget the lines you wrote?"

Of course not. They're Holden's lines to Opal. I just never thought someone would be reciting them to me. I feel a little shiver go through me.

"Excuse me," I stammer. "I've got to get this punch back."

Simon reaches out and touches my arm. "You can't run away forever, Marie," he says. "Sooner or later you're going to have to face things."

What things, exactly? I want to ask, but now is not the time. Simon doesn't seem to be aware of it, or maybe he just doesn't care, but we are fast becoming the center of attention. I get away from him before we give the school gossips something new to gnaw on.

The rest of the night passes in a blur. I don't talk to Simon anymore, but I see him from time to time, either talking to people or dancing with one of the sophomore girls from the Thespians. He dances with her twice, both times fast ones.

127

I feel very much on edge and kind of giddy. It's all I can do to sit still. I keep thinking about Simon, only a few feet away, and how he must have come to this dance just to see me. It really boggles my mind to think about it.

Of course I try to act as normal as possible around Brian and everybody else. But Brian isn't about to let Simon's unexpected appearance go by without comment — he lets me know in no uncertain terms how displeased he is. I try to remember that he's got a broken leg, that he's depressed, and that normally he's a really sweet guy. But he doesn't let up, and then I start to get angry. I swear, if it weren't for the fact that I detest making scenes, I think I'd break up with him right here and now.

But somehow I manage to hold my temper and answer him as sweetly as I can. It's just too tacky for words to break up with your boyfriend — your *injured* boyfriend — the night of the St. Valentine's Day dance.

Inside, though, I know I can't put it off forever.

Nine

"What I can't figure out is why you just didn't tell Brian to go get stuffed," Tina tells me the next day at her house. She shakes her head. "There you were, presented with the perfect opportunity to discard one boyfriend and pick up another, killing two birds with one stone, so to speak, and you blew it."

"Tina, I wish you wouldn't joke about this."

She sighs. "Okay. But you're going to have to face it sooner or later, just like Simon said. Or you could do what you usually do — get Brian to break up with you, and make him think it's all his idea."

"What?"

"Like you did with Kevin and then with David before him, remember? You wanted to get rid of them before they wanted to get rid of you, so you just kept getting them angry until they had to break it off. It's so strange, Marie — most girls would rather *die* than admit they're the ones who got dumped, and you're just the opposite."

I think about what she said, and after a minute I have to concede that she's right. Unfortunately she usually is.

"I guess it's easier that way," I tell her, shrugging.

"Maybe you have some sort of martyr complex."

I groan. "Tina, if you don't stop watching those talk shows you're going to end up a *genius*."

"I know. I'm so smart as it is that sometimes I just can't stand myself!"

I throw a pillow at her.

The student council is selling carnations for Valentine's Day. You pay a dollar, and they bring a carnation to the person of your choice during homeroom. I'm not expecting any because Brian wasn't in school last week, and anyway, he hasn't exactly been in a romantic mood lately. I doubt if he'll even give me a card, although I've bought one for him, just in case.

So imagine my surprise when I get not one carnation, but twelve, all red, and with no message. Not that I need one. I can pretty well guess who sent them.

I try to look nonchalant, as if I get a dozen carnations every day of my life. But inside I'm kind of thrilled. What a romantic gesture! I'm also kind of nervous — if Brian hears about this. . . .

Naturally, Brian does hear, and he is *ticked off* about it. He's waiting for me at lunch, as usual, and I haven't even sat down before he's demanding who sent them to me.

"I did," says Tina, stepping in. "It's a tradition. Each

130

year we send each other flowers, just in case *nobody else does*." She gives him this significant look. "It's kind of a morale booster."

It's obvious that Brian doesn't believe her, but it's also obvious that he's not going to call her a liar to her face. "You sent *twelve?*"

She shrugs. "I got carried away."

Just then, a couple of giggling sophomore girls come up and ask Brian if they can sign his cast. That takes his attention away from me right up until the bell rings.

"Thanks," I whisper to Tina on the way out. "You saved me."

"Yeah, but I might not be around next time to do it," she whispers back.

Oh, how right she is. Brian is waiting for me by my locker after school — and this time, Tina is nowhere around. He insists that I walk him to the parking lot, where I see Josh waiting for him in his car.

He starts going on about how I never have time for him anymore (never mind that I spent all last week nursing him back to health), and how I'm always doing stuff with the play (he actually said "stupid play") and about how bad it looks for me to be spending so much time with "that jerk," and how humiliating it is for him to have his supposed girlfriend get a dozen carnations practically in front of the whole school, and how nobody believes they were from Tina. He goes on and on, point by point (I think he's been coached by Josh), and then he ends the whole spiel by telling me that either I stop having anything to do with the play or we're through.

"If that's what you really want," I tell him, sighing.

Brian looks smug. His face breaks out into this huge

131

grin. Then he notices me reaching up behind my neck to unclasp the necklace he gave me for Christmas, and he isn't grinning anymore.

"No, don't say anything else," I say, dropping the necklace into his hand. "I know you can't control the way you feel, Brian. It's not your fault. I don't blame you."

"Marie — "

"No, no, don't make it any harder for me," I say, holding up my hands and trying to look brave. "I know you're sorry, and you still want to be friends. I'll try, Brian, honestly I will, but it won't be easy."

"But Marie — "

"Good-bye, Brian," I tell him sadly but firmly, and then I walk away as fast as my legs can carry me before he can realize what hit him.

I needn't have worried; I look out of the corner of my eye and see him standing there, holding the necklace, with this truly dumbfounded expression on his face.

Now it's my turn to feel smug, only what I'm feeling is closer to relief. It's over, and I think I handled it very smoothly. I've let Brian save face, so he can't get mad at me. For the first few days he'll feel bad about breaking my heart, but I don't let it bother me. I figure a little remorse won't hurt him any.

I drive home and find Mom in her room, packing for a business trip to Los Angeles.

"Brian and I just broke up," I tell her, and her brow wrinkles in a frown. She pulls me onto the bed next to her.

"I'm sorry, honey."

I shrug. "I'm okay."

"Sure you are," she says, giving me a hug. "And you know, you may not believe me now, but this is really for the best. As much as your father and I liked Brian, I always felt he restricted you. You're just beginning to become your own person, to branch out and test your wings. Finding out you weren't right for each other was inevitable."

I nod, staying silent.

"Are you sure you're all right?" she asks. "Do you want to talk about it?"

I shake my head. I feel sneaky, getting all this sympathy when all I'm really worried about is how I'm going to go out with Simon without Brian finding out and making life difficult. The whole thing is too complicated to explain to my mother, though.

"It's just that everything's so difficult," I tell her. "I thought things would start to get easier by now."

Mom laughs, giving me another hug. "Just wait until you get older, honey," she says.

Is that a threat?

I think long and carefully about what I should do, and then I decide not to do anything. I don't want to start dating again right away, anyway. That would be too tacky.

I go to rehearsals the next day and act like nothing's happened. The funny thing is, that's the way everybody else is acting, too. I figure that either the Thespians are too wrapped up in the play to pay attention to the gossip that is quickly spreading through the halls of Magothy High like a new strain of virus, or they're just too polite to remark on my newly single status.

I don't say anything to Simon — I don't even thank

him for the flowers. (Well, I don't know for *sure* that he sent them, do I?) But I think he's too tense about the technical rehearsals that we've been having all week to notice.

Everybody's tense, and not without reason. So far, everything that can go wrong has gone wrong. First the lights don't work right. They get the lights working, and then the audio goes on the blink. They get the lights and the audio working right, and then the scenery falls down right on top of Opal and Holden during their love scene.

It would be kind of funny, and we all might have a good laugh if Simon weren't snarling at everyone like a rabid dog.

"Need I remind you people that we open in exactly ten days?" he shouts. He is really playing the anguished artist to the hilt. Not for the first time I feel a tinge of regret that he didn't cast himself as Holden. He'd be great, especially when Holden starts to flip out — he wouldn't even have to act that part.

Of course we don't need reminding that the play opens in ten days. Let's say we couldn't read the posters that are up all over the school, and somehow missed the announcements that are made every morning in homeroom. There's *no* way on earth we could ignore Simon bellowing like the voice of doom every day, as he counts down the remaining hours until showtime.

Quite honestly, Simon is being so impossible that I'm surprised the technical crew hasn't walked out on him. Followed in close succession by the actors, because he's not treating them so nicely, either. Even I'm having second thoughts about him.

"It's just nerves," Beverly tells me confidingly. "The

director always comes unglued the closer we get to opening night. You watch. Next week we have dress rehearsals. It'll be the actors' turn then."

Oh, joy. An entire room full of screaming lunatics. I can hardly wait.

The scenes with the river turn out to be particularly tricky, just as I predicted. The people who hold the material, while simulating waves, just aren't getting it right.

"No, no, no!" Simon shouts, jumping onstage. "You're not waving a flag! You're supposed to be a flowing river — so flow!" He takes one end of the material and starts showing them.

"What are you grinning about, Carrie?" he snaps to one of the girls holding the material. She immediately turns stone-faced. "Don't smile, don't frown, don't show any emotion whatsoever — you're *supposed* to be inanimate! The audience shouldn't notice you at all!"

I think Simon just made what they call a tactical error. Nobody likes to be told that while they're having their big moment on stage, no one is going to notice them.

"No, no, no!" Simon is shouting what seems like several hours later. Max and Adam are onstage doing the final scene, where Holden finally kills his uncle.

"Holden — " Simon always calls the actors by their character's name during rehearsals — "remember that you're angry, boiling angry, crazy angry! Remember that this is the man who killed your father and knows your secret! You're not only killing him, you're killing that terrible secret! You were glad when your father died, and he knows it! You don't want anyone else to know it, right?"

135

Adam nods weakly, and my heart goes out to him. Simon has been hardest on him. The poor guy looks like he's been put through a meat grinder.

"You've got to put your hands around his neck like so." Simon puts his hands around Max's neck. He's looking at Adam, so he misses the expression on Max's face. "Then you really choke him, get it? Really let him have it!"

Max, meanwhile, starts to make strangling noises.

"Uh, Simon — " he gasps, and Simon glances back at him.

"Good, Claude!" He pats Max, who is having a coughing fit, on the back. "The way you rolled your eyes — a look of absolute terror. Keep it up!"

The rest of us exchange looks. I'm pretty sure that Max wasn't completely acting.

It's pretty late when we finally finish for the day. Everybody is beat, but I have to admit the scenes are better. Simon's intensity seems to have rubbed off on the actors. Or maybe it's just his threats.

The rest of the week goes about the same: Simon unhappy about everything, and everybody, including me, staying out of his way.

At least I try to stay out of his way. He corners me at one point during a rehearsal break.

"Don't you have any opinions to contribute?" he demands. "You're supposed to be a member of this team, you know!"

I stare at him, flabbergasted. Usually I would walk away — I mean, I've already contributed my part, haven't I? But today — today, I've had it with Simon and his tyrannical ways! To think I broke up with one of the greatest guys in the whole school for this creep!

136

"Oh, really?" I say sarcastically. "I thought it was a one-man show, with you as the head ham! Get stuffed, Simon."

I expect him really to let me have it, and I'm ready. I feel my face get hot and my hands clench by my side.

He just stands there, looking at me, and suddenly he starts grinning. It starts slowly, getting bigger, until pretty soon that grin reaches from ear to ear.

The funny thing is, I want to grin back.

Simon starts acting more like a human being after that. Or maybe I just don't let him get to me so much. Anyway, things start going more smoothly, and I start to relax. I'm starting to think that everything will work out for the best after all.

I'm feeling particularly good on Friday, when I'm sitting at home, innocent as you please. Then the phone rings.

"Why didn't you tell me you broke up with the jock?" Simon demands straight off.

"I didn't think it was any of your business."

I wish I could take it back the moment I've said it, because of course I don't mean it. It's just that he's really caught me off guard, attacking me like that.

There's silence on the other end of the phone. "Give me one good reason why I shouldn't hang up this phone right now," says Simon.

I start thinking. "Don't hang up," I tell him.

"Then stop playing games with me, Marie. What are you doing tonight?"

"Baby-sitting."

"Right. Pull the other one."

"I am." I feel like laughing, but I know Simon would

think that I'm laughing at him even though I'm really laughing at the situation. "You can come over if you like," I offer. "They're friends of my parents — they won't mind."

"Should I pick you up or meet you there?"

"Pick me up. Around seven-thirty, if that's okay with you."

"I'll be there," he says, and it sounds like a threat. I hang up the phone and wonder what I'm getting myself into.

I don't wonder about it too much, because I've got to change my clothes.

The Rubinsteins are this very yuppie couple, who just had a baby last year. His name is Benjamin and he is really cute. But what a handful!

I remember their house before — very elegant and clean, with all the latest in stereo equipment and kitchen gadgets. Now there are toys strewn everywhere, and the place looks like a tornado hit it. I remember what the Rubinsteins looked like before — thin, in shape, dressed like models from *Vogue* and *GQ*, always going off to play tennis or vacationing in Europe. Now she looks tired all the time, her clothes aren't so nice, and she's got a set of saddlebags that just won't budge. It's worse for him — he's starting to go bald! It makes you wonder about having babies, if this is what just one little baby can do to you.

Benjamin is already asleep when we get there. (Do I know how to pick baby-sitting jobs or don't I?) I listen while Mrs. Rubinstein tells me about a zillion things I might have to do if the baby wakes up. She gives me about a hundred telephone numbers, and points out everything we can help ourselves to in the kitchen.

Then they leave. Right away I look at Simon and say, "Listen, I don't want to start dating again too soon. I think I need to give it some time."

This is pretty brave and mature, coming from me, but all Simon says is, "You worry too much about what other people think."

"Maybe so. But I don't want to go out with anyone at least until the play is over."

"Fair enough. We're going to have too much to do from now until then, in any case. Is that why you didn't tell me you and the jock were through? You were afraid I'd come over and drag you out with me or something?"

That's basically exactly what I thought, but I would sound awfully conceited to say so. "Did you send those carnations to make trouble?" I ask him instead, and he gives me a blank look.

"What carnations?"

But then he starts to laugh, and I realize he's teasing. Which is a good thing, because it would just be too complicated if I were to find out that I really do have a secret admirer.

"Come on, let's get something to eat," he says.

We go into the kitchen, and I pour us some milk and make peanut butter sandwiches. (The Rubinsteins are really into peanut butter these days.) I sit down at the kitchen table with Simon and watch him devour the food, and I start to have this fantasy about us being married and this being our house and little Benjamin upstairs being our baby. Then I start to think that fantasizing like that is pretty sick, considering we haven't even been on a date yet.

"What are you staring at?" Simon asks, eating his second sandwich.

"I just didn't know you liked peanut butter so much," I lie.

"There's a lot you don't know about me."

"Like what?"

"Like I hate to fly, I'm allergic to strawberries, and" — he finishes off his milk — "I'm a really good bowler."

That cracks me up. I start laughing so hard that Simon starts to look annoyed. "What's so funny?"

"You — bowling!" I tell him. "I can't believe you like to bowl!"

"I don't like it all that much, but I am good at it."

That's a relief, because I don't see myself ever getting to like bowling any better than I do now. "I thought you were the type to go for long walks in the woods," I tell him.

"That's nice," he agrees. "Look, Marie, you seem to have a lot of preconceived notions about me. It's not a good idea to make snap assumptions about people the minute you meet them, you know."

"You should talk. You made all kinds of assumptions the first time you met me. Be honest — what was the first thing that passed through your mind the very first time you saw me?"

"The very first time I saw you was in Mrs. Mason's class last year."

"Oh, right, I forgot about that. And the first thing you thought was 'airhead,' right?"

He shakes his head. "The very first thing I thought was, 'Wow, she's pretty.' "

My heart starts that crazy thumping again. "Get serious," I say, aiming for lightness.

"I am serious," he says very seriously. "The second thing I thought was that I liked your smile and the way your hair is so dark and your skin so white, and the way your dress rides up when you cross your legs — "

"Hey!" I punch him in the arm, and he laughs.

"You were going out with a jock then, too. You were always dating jocks."

"I'm not anymore," I remind him.

"Yeah." He gets this smile on his face, and that's when I decide it's a good time to look in on little Benjamin.

When I get back, he's washed the dishes we used and is poking around by the VCR, checking out all the tapes.

"All they have is *Sesame Street* and tapes of the baby," he complains.

"I brought something to watch with me," I tell him, and hand him my copy of you-know-what.

"*Home from the Hill*," he reads. "I've never heard of it."

"Good. That means you haven't seen it already."

I figure Simon just passed some sort of test. A lot of guys would insist on turning on the TV and watching some stupid and senselessly violent cop show. Simon has just proved to me that he at least has an open mind. He sets up the videotape while I make us some popcorn in the microwave.

The movie starts, and it isn't very long before Simon is saying, "This is pretty dumb." But he keeps watching it anyway. Especially the part where George Hamilton is making out with his girlfriend in the woods. That's when Simon lets out this big yawn, putting his arm around me at the same time. I guess the yawn is to keep me from noticing the arm around the back of the sofa. Do guys think we're totally stupid?

In the old days they used to fade out the love scenes, so you're not sure what's happened until you realize that George Hamilton's girlfriend needs to get married — quick — and that old George is not interested in tying the knot. Then George Peppard, his illegitimate half-brother, steps in and offers to marry her, and I find that very, very romantic.

"This is really dumb," says Simon, but I can tell he's hooked. Boys always say romantic things are dumb. It's a macho thing. My brothers are supercritical about the soaps I watch, but I notice that they seem to know all the characters' names and the story lines.

The movie ends, and I go upstairs to check on Benjamin again. Then we start to watch this horror movie on cable. It's supposed to be scary, but it's too stupid to be anything but boring. I can see Simon thinks the same. I feel like he's passed another test.

After a while my mind starts to wander. I think about the two of us sitting on the sofa, so comfortable, an empty bowl of popcorn between us, looking like an old married couple like the Rubinsteins. It's so different from what I imagined our first date would be, that I have to laugh.

"What's so funny?" Simon asks, startled. On the

screen the actors are meeting one grisly death after another.

I shake my head, not wanting to tell him. Then I remember the New Year's Eve party and how Tina and I had tried to guess what Simon was doing. I almost ask him if he dates college girls, but stop myself just in time.

"Do you like poetry?" I ask instead.

"Poetry?" Simon lifts that eyebrow in a way I now find totally endearing. "Some of it, but not much."

I'm glad to hear it. Simon is right — I did make assumptions about him without really knowing him. I make a silent promise to myself never to let that happen again.

Simon nudges me with his elbow. "Are you going to share the joke?"

Smiling, I say, "It's just that this isn't the way I imagined our first date to be."

"Oh, so this is a date?"

Too late I realize my mistake. "No, not a date — "

But then Simon is kissing me. And is it a great kiss! Just like I remember.

"Do you always kiss without warning like that?" I demand when he lets me go.

He looks amused. "Should I sound an alarm first?"

"Well, it would be a change."

"Okay, I'm warning you now. This is a date, and on dates you sometimes get kissed, so be on the alert — "

And then he starts kissing me again. And it is even better than before. It goes on and on until I think I'm going to die, it's so wonderful. Really the most wonderful kiss I've ever had.

Then we hear the key in the lock, and we have to pull ourselves together, if you know what I mean. But Simon is smiling at me, kind of a goofy smile, and there's this twinkle in his eyes. He is so gorgeous! How could I ever have thought otherwise?

Simon drives me home. I'm half expecting a major tussle in the car, but he very politely gets out and walks me to the door. He doesn't lunge for me there, either. He just gives me a very solemn kiss on the forehead.

"Good-night, Marie," he says, touching my cheek. "I'll see you on Monday."

I float upstairs to my room, thinking that this was the nicest non-date I've ever had. Maybe the nicest time, date or non-date, that I've ever had with any boy, period. I'm kicking myself for making such a fuss about not dating, because now I'll have to wait two whole days before I can see Simon again.

Or maybe I'll call him up before then.

I think I'm falling in love.

Ten

I've been avoiding Ashley and her crowd ever since Brian and I broke up. I figure it's better to give them the cold shoulder before they can give it to me. Besides, I know Ashley's still miffed about not getting the part of Opal in the play.

So naturally, when she corners me alone in the girls' bathroom on Monday, acting like we're long lost sisters, I'm suspicious.

"I've been trying to talk to you for ages!" she squeals, giving me a little hug. "I want you to know how sorry I am about you and Brian."

"Uh — that's okay," I tell her. I glance around the stalls, figuring I'm being set up for some kind of cruel joke.

"Josh asked me to fix Brian up with one of my

friends," Ashley says, "but I told him to forget it. Like, no way could I do that to you."

I don't know whether to thank her or not, so I don't say anything. This sure is one weird conversation.

"Then I heard he went out with Hollie Winningham Saturday night," she tells me, nearly spitting the name. Hollie Winningham is this very sexy-looking girl with a pretty bad reputation, or a pretty good one, depending on your point of view. Needless to say, the girls hate her, but the boys seem to think she's great — which is probably why the girls hate her so much. I don't really know her that well, but she seems all right. Not the kind of girl Brian usually goes out with, but maybe he wanted a change. She's certainly nothing like me.

"I heard someone saw them in the McDonald's parking lot at about two o'clock in the morning, making out like crazy," Ashley says. "Like, how sleazy can you get?"

This is surprising news, but I figure most of it's just rumor. "I hope they had a good time," I tell her, but it's obvious she thinks I'm just putting on an act.

"I think he did it to make you jealous," she tells me.

"Ashley, that doesn't make sense."

She nods emphatically. "Yes, it does. He's sorry he broke it off with you. Really sorry, so now he's using Hollie to make you jealous. Why else would he go out with her?"

I could think of lots of reasons, but I stay silent. Ashley is studying me very intently.

"Are you? Like, jealous?"

I shake my head. "Absolutely not."

"Not the teeniest bit?"

"Not the teeniest bit."

"Sure?"

"Positive." I look her straight in the face. "Not even the teeny-weeniest itsy-bitsiest bit jealous. He can go out with all the girls he wants. I hope he does. Why shouldn't he have some fun? I *want* him to have fun. Honestly, Ashley, I am not even remotely jealous."

She gives me this very self-satisfied nod. "You're jealous," she says, and I sigh. Sometimes people only hear what they want to hear.

"Well, don't worry; he'll come back. I'll make sure all the girls give him the freeze until he does."

"Ashley, I really wish you wouldn't do that."

"Don't thank me," she says breezily. "What are friends for?"

"Please, Ashley," I begin, but she's already out the door. After taking one last look in the mirror, of course.

I feel like I'm caught in some bizarre nightmare from *The Twilight Zone*. I can't figure Ashley out at all. Why should she care if Brian and I break up? I'd always figured she'd have Brian lined up with one of her cheerleading friends in two seconds flat the minute we broke up.

Maybe it's just that, being a manipulative person, she likes to be the one pulling the strings, telling people when they can break up and when they have to stay together. Maybe she just likes doubling with Brian and me. Maybe she just prefers me to Hollie Winningham.

Maybe she's just trying to be nice. Doing what a good friend would do. Hey, anything is possible.

I think about this all morning, and by the afternoon I still haven't come up with any definite answers. Finally I tell myself to stop worrying about it and to be happy. Now that Brian has been seen publicly on a date with another girl, I can safely go out with Simon.

Tina's waiting for me in Spanish class with this very urgent look on her face.

"You'll never guess what!" she says, grasping my arm. "It's so dramatic, I can't stand it! Simon and Brian had a fight!"

"What?" I stare at her, flabbergasted. "Where? When? What happened?"

She shakes her head. "I don't know. They had a fight, that's all I heard."

"*Buenas tardes, alumnos,*" Mrs. Alvarez intones from the front of the class. Tina gives me a helpless shrug before turning around in her seat.

"*Buenas tardes, Señora Alvarez,*" the class answers back. Everyone except me. Horrible images of Simon with a black eye, a bloody nose, a head squashed like a melon, are running through my head. A fight! How could Brian and Simon have a fight? I thought I'd handled everything so smoothly!

I'm worrying so much that I consider asking Mrs. Alvarez for a pass to the office. Maybe somebody there could tell me what happened. But then Mrs. Alvarez calls on me to conjugate some verb, and I have no idea what she's talking about. She gets all offended that I haven't been paying attention — like there's nothing more important than some stupid Spanish verb — and picks on me throughout the entire class.

I don't see Simon until after school. By this time I'm crazy with worry.

"What happened?" I cry, scrutinizing his face. There don't seem to be any cuts or bruises. Maybe he's got them elsewhere.

"When?" Simon asks, looking confused.

"What do you mean, when? I heard you and Brian had a fight!"

Simon laughs. Really hard. "That's the power of rumor for you."

"Oh. You mean you didn't have a fight?"

He shakes his head. "No, we passed each other in the hall. I think he muttered something under his breath."

"That's *it*?"

"Yep. Hey, you look disappointed. Did you think he was going to challenge me to a duel?"

"No — "

"But you did think he was going to beat me to a pulp."

"Of course not," I lie, because that's exactly what I thought. But I suddenly realize that I'm not being very complimentary towards Simon. No boy wants the girl he likes to think he's anything less than Sylvester Stallone, Arnold Schwarzenegger, and Hulk Hogan all rolled into one. Boys are very sensitive about their so-called virility. It's another one of those macho things.

"I can take care of myself, you know."

"Of course you can," I say quickly. "It's just that I was worried — "

" — because you thought he was going to beat me

to a pulp," Simon finishes for me. "Look, it's okay, Marie. I know I'm not exactly a Rambo-type of guy, so stop trying to *appease* me, will you? You're way too obvious to get away with it."

"Get away with what?" I ask sharply.

"You know, that cutesy act of yours. First you open your eyes real wide and innocent, and then your voice goes all soft and sugary-sweet, and anybody with half a brain can see you're lying. That crap worked with the jock, but it doesn't fly with me."

"Well, I'm *sorry* I was concerned about you."

"Don't be sorry. That part I kind of like." He smiles. "But you don't have to worry. I can handle myself even if I don't have biceps the size of large pineapples. Okay?"

"Okay," I repeat, and this time I mean it. Simon is so smart and so self-confident — of course he can handle himself. "It's just that I don't like fighting," I explain. "I don't like any kind of violence at all. It's so . . . unpleasant."

He laughs again, putting an arm around me. "You sound just like my grandmother."

I pull back, giving him a look to kill.

"But you don't look like her," he adds, grinning. We start towards the auditorium, but he stops right outside the doors.

"Brian does know it's over, right?" It's the first time I've ever heard him call Brian by his name. "He doesn't think that there's some chance for the two of you getting back together?"

"Of course not!" I answer vehemently. Maybe a shade too vehemently, but Simon looks satisfied. Maybe that time I wasn't so obvious.

"Good." He opens the door for me. "Come on, we've got a lot of work to do."

This is the final week of rehearsals. Five days before D-day. Five days of dress rehearsals, which, in my humble opinion, go even worse than the technical rehearsals did.

We're getting down to the wire now and, just like Beverly said, everybody is super-tense. The actors and crew snap at each other continually and go into rages over the most trivial things.

Simon, believe it or not, has become the one voice of reason in this loony bin. He's remarkably calm. Tina says this is due to me. I think it's more likely due to his perverse leadership style, but I don't argue with Tina. Right now I'm just too grateful that *somebody*, at least, is keeping a clear head. Everybody else is falling apart, and that includes the playwright. I'm a nervous wreck.

Forget the actors, the props, the lights, the audio — all of that is just the icing on the cake. The play itself is the crucial thing. I mean, the greatest actors in the world can't make a bad play good, can they? What if the audience laughs? I will just die if they laugh. What if they think it's stupid? What if they just plain hate it? What if they start to boo and throw tomatoes?

"I think you're on the verge of hysteria," Simon tells me. "No one is going to boo and throw tomatoes. They don't do that anymore, not even in a real theater."

"Oh, so they'll just *want* to boo and throw tomatoes?" I ask. "That's some comfort, I suppose."

Simon chuckles, the fiend. I'm a nervous wreck, and he's chuckling like Bozo the clown.

"Don't worry," he tells me.

"Such sterling advice. Gee, thanks."

"No, seriously, Marie, this play is going to be a hit. The first of many. Years from now, when you're a world-famous playwright, people will say, 'I was there when it all began. I was there at Marie Valpacchio's first opening night!' "

"Unfortunately she didn't survive it to enjoy her success," I finish for him. Simon gives my shoulder a reassuring squeeze.

"You'll survive. You'll survive, and we'll both go on to bigger and better things. I figure this will be just the first of our many collaborations. We'll be the famous directing-playwriting team. All over Broadway, you'll see our names in lights" — he gestures with his hands, imagining some huge, neon-lit marquee — "Conreith and Valpacchio!"

"You mean, *Valpacchio* and Conreith."

He sighs. "Cripes, already she's demanding star billing. Where did you learn to be so temperamental?"

"I had the best teacher," I tell him pointedly. Simon just laughs.

The Thursday night dress rehearsal is a disaster. I mean, a complete, total, absolute, no-question-about-it disaster. Simon says I'm exaggerating. He says my hysteria is influencing my judgment.

"Don't worry," he tells me. "A bad dress rehearsal always means a good opening night. It's a tradition."

I stare at him in amazement. Only last week he was a crazed maniac, and now he's Mr. Cool. I tell you, it's not natural!

"If that's true, then we should have the best opening

night in the history of theater," I say, and Simon just laughs again.

I feel sick to my stomach. Really sick.

Everyone I know is coming to the play on Friday night. I have so many relatives coming — from both sides — that I'm afraid there won't be any room for anybody else. Even my brothers are making a special trip down from college, but I figure they also have laundry to do.

And then it's opening night. Suddenly all the joking, the wisecracking, the fooling around, and even the bickering, is over. Everyone is shaking with nerves, and the smiles they exchange are grimaces of terror. No kidding, everyone is dead serious.

Mom got me a new dress to wear tonight, and I go to the girls' room to make sure it's hanging right. Looking in the mirror, I hear the horrible sound of someone throwing up.

I stand there, not knowing what to do. Then I see Sabrina stagger out, looking rather green underneath her stage makeup.

"Oh, my God, Sabrina!" I exclaim. "Are you all right?"

She nods weakly. "Yeah, it's okay. I can still go on."

I feel a rush of relief and then an equal rush of guilt. Here I am worrying about the play, when Sabrina is sick!

"Are you sure?" I ask, not really wanting to know if she's not. We need Sabrina. No understudy could touch her performance as Grace.

"I'm sure," she tells me, managing a smile. "Don't look so worried. This always happens to me."

"Always? You mean every time you have to go on stage, you — "

She nods. "Every time."

I stare at her, speechless. Sabrina has been in an awful lot of plays. I can't believe she gets sick like this before every one. How gross! Why does she stick with it?

I begin to wonder if the boys are getting sick, too. And then I start to worry about our Opal. After making sure Sabrina is okay, I go looking for Deirdre.

Backstage is in total chaos, with everyone shouting orders and running around like chickens without heads, but I do eventually find Deirdre. She's sitting quietly, methodically biting her nails down to the quick. Beneath the makeup, I can already see a sheen of perspiration.

"Ready to go on?" I ask her brightly.

"As I'll ever be," she tells me, and goes back to what's left of her nails.

It's almost curtain time, so I start to make my way down to the audience, where my parents are saving me a seat. Simon grabs my hand before I can go.

"Stick around," he says. "We might need your help."

I don't see how I can **be** of any help. In fact, I'm sure I'll just be in the way. But then Simon gives me this sort of pleading look and I notice his hands are sweaty. He must be as nervous as everybody else, I realize, only it's worse for him. He can't show it. He's got to be a rock, because we're all depending upon him.

154

I squeeze his hand. "No problem," I say, and he smiles.

Five minutes later the curtain opens and *Holden, The Prince of Culpeper County* begins. I wish I could say that I'm enjoying it, but the truth is, I'm not even paying attention to it. I'm pacing back and forth, trying to stay out of everybody's way, anxiously waiting for the sounds of laughter.

I don't hear any. After a while I take a peek out at the audience. Nobody is sneering in disgust. Nobody is yawning, coughing, picking their nose, or doing any of the things that usually signal acute boredom. Mostly they look pretty interested. Not bored at all.

I start to watch the play from the wings. And then I start to feel the rhythm of the dialogue, the pacing, all the things that make good drama. A few minutes later, I realize that it's a good play. Maybe a great play, and the actors are out there making it come alive! It's a miracle. It's a wonderful, magical, amazing miracle, and it's *mine*!

Well, mostly mine.

In no time at all, it's over. The audience is clapping furiously, and the actors are taking their bows. Then the actors start clapping for Simon, who comes out, bringing the technical crew behind him. And then *everybody* starts clapping and chanting "Author! Author!"

Wait a minute! That's me!

I stand there, petrified, and then Simon comes and drags me onstage. It's like a dream. Someone is pressing roses into my arms, the audience is on their feet, cheering, "Author! Author!" and then *I'm* taking a bow!

I'm hooked. Now I know why Sabrina puts up with getting sick before every performance, and why Deirdre puts up with chewed-up nails, and why everyone is willing to work until they practically pass out from exhaustion. The sound of that applause makes it every bit worthwhile. I can see why people say applause is addictive. It is.

I'll tell you something else, something I haven't admitted to anyone, even to myself, until this very minute. *I* worked hard on this play, right from the beginning. I didn't write it in one weekend, on the spur of the moment, like I told everyone. I put a lot of hours, a lot of sweat, and a lot of *me* into this play, and that's the truth.

Okay, so maybe I'm not so lazy after all. I guess it's not a crime.

The curtain goes down, and then we're all hugging each other and crying, even the boys. I find myself next to Adam, who is still pale and sweating, but I give him a hug anyway. I feel glad for him. I know how anxious he was for this to all be over. I know how sorry he was he ever tried out for the play.

At least I think I know. "You were fabulous!" I shout.

He grins. "I was, wasn't I?"

"But there's still tomorrow," I remind him.

He doesn't look worried. There's a gleam in his eye that tells me he's looking forward to tomorrow and to all the performances after that. Adam's hooked, too.

"How about some of that for me?" I hear a low voice growl behind me. I turn and give the director a hug that would suffocate a grizzly bear.

Simon hugs me back so hard he almost lifts me off the ground.

"Pretty good, huh?" he says, laughing.

"*Good?*" I repeat, amazed. "It was *great!* It was fantastic, tremendous, magnificent! It was absolutely *wonderful!*"

I keep babbling on until I run out of adjectives to describe how truly incredible it was. This takes some time, because, you know, words *are* sort of my specialty. But Simon doesn't seem to mind. He's so happy, I don't think he even hears me.

Pretty soon there are so many people backstage that it's hard to breathe. It's like a party, and I'm one of the guests of honor. Everybody is there to congratulate me. Tina and Mike, Tina's parents, my parents, my brothers, and about a hundred of my relatives. I introduce Simon to them and then want to die when my Grandmother Valpacchio calls him a "cute boy" and pinches his cheek! Simon takes it pretty well, though. He introduces me to his family. They seem nice and not nearly so embarrassing as mine.

Then everybody starts to leave, everybody except us, because we're going to Sabrina's house for an opening-night celebration. There's a lot more hugging and kissing, but soon after that, the cast and crew are all that's left. We start to clean up and get ourselves ready.

I go into the bathroom one last time to comb my hair and check my face. I'm in a hurry. Simon is waiting for me. We're going to drive to Sabrina's house together. Our first official date.

But when I come out of the bathroom, instead of Simon I find Brian, of all people, standing there, leaning on his crutch.

157

"Brian!" I exclaim. "What are you doing here?"

"I came with some other people . . . they left." He shifts his weight so that he's leaning against the wall. "I waited around. I wanted to talk to you."

"Gee, Brian, I'm pretty busy right now."

"It'll only take a minute."

I sigh and glance around the empty corridor. It doesn't look like I'm going to get out of this.

"Look, I know you're sore at me," Brian says hurriedly. "I don't blame you, I know I really hurt you a lot — "

"Oh, that's okay," I tell him, which I guess sounds pretty stupid, because he stops. I think I've spoiled his concentration.

"I know I hurt you," he begins again, "but I still care about you, Marie. I know you feel the same, and now that this is all over and you've gotten this drama thing out of your system, well, I want you to be my girlfriend again." He looks at me. "You know, like it was before."

"That's not possible, Brian," I tell him as gently as I can. Which isn't easy, because I am just dying to get out of here. Simon is waiting for me, I don't want to be a part of this uncomfortable scene, and it hasn't escaped my notice that Brian is pretty much talking like a selfish pig. I mean, I'd have to be *insane* to want to go back to things the way they were before.

Furthermore, he hasn't said one word about my wonderful play! Which is the real reason, I guess, why I'm not feeling as sympathetic toward him as I should.

Brian just nods, as though he expected me to put up a fight. "Yeah, Ashley told me you were mad about

158

me going out with Hollie. It didn't mean anything, Marie — "

"Brian, please don't say that. It's not fair — "

"I've got something for you," he says, grasping my hand. He takes out the little silver necklace. It dangles in the light before he places my fingers around it. "I'd put it on for you if I could," he says jokingly. "Please say you'll wear it, Marie."

"Oh, Brian — " He can be so sweet sometimes. I shake my head. "I can't. I'm sorry, but I can't do that." I take a step closer to him and place the necklace in his shirt pocket. "I'm really sorry, Brian," I repeat sadly. "I hope we can still be friends."

Brian gives me the same look he had the time he was sacked during football practice from behind, just when he thought he was home free. Like somebody had just punched him, hard, when he was least expecting it. I guess in a way somebody had.

I lean over and kiss his cheek. It's a good-bye kind of peck, but Brian isn't ready to give up yet.

"If you'd just listen to me for a second," he says, grabbing my arm. "If you'd just let me explain about Hollie — "

But I'm not listening to him. I'm staring at Simon, who is staring at us. He's to the back of Brian, but I can see his face; he looks like he's been punched, too. Punched so hard that the wind's been knocked out of him. I open my mouth to speak, but he's already turning away and walking toward the door.

I pull my hand out of Brian's grasp. "Please try to understand," I say, interrupting his long explanation about Hollie. "It doesn't matter about Hollie. I'm sorry, but I'm just not interested in you that way any-more. You're a great guy and everything, but it's over."

"But I thought you said — "

"I was wrong," I cut in quickly. "I should have told you how I really felt before, but I didn't. I thought letting you think what you wanted to think would be easier, but now I know that was a mistake. I'm sorry."

For a minute Brian just stares at me, dumbfounded, and then his face clouds in anger. "I get it — this is about that Conreith jerk, right? He's been moving in on you all along, hasn't he? Man, when I get this cast off — "

"Brian," I say loudly. As bad as I feel for him, it's all I can do not to scream in frustration. "This has nothing to do with Simon or Hollie, or with anybody at all, except us. We're just not right for each other. Think about it, and you'll see what I mean, really you will."

"I see plenty!" He scowls. "This is it, Marie, no playing around. I warn you, you walk away now and you walk away for good. We're finished. I'm not about to beg for any girl."

I nod my head, wishing it didn't have to be like this. I feel pretty heartless and cold. Definitely not nice. But I know I did the right thing. I know it's better for him to be angry with me now than to be going around still thinking we might get back together.

I start to walk away.

"Hey, wait a minute!"

"I'm sorry, I can't." I give him a smile that means good-bye. "Take care of yourself, Brian. Be happy."

I leave him there, leaning against his crutch, know-ing he can't run after me. I see Hollie slinking behind

160

a corner, and I'm pretty sure Brian will be all right. Unless Hollie heard what he said about her.

But I can't spend any more time worrying about Brian. I've already done enough of that. Now I have to find Simon.

I look everywhere for him, but he's gone. Everybody is gone. The auditorium is deserted. I'm beginning to think I'm going to have to call my parents to come pick me up, and then I spot Beverly. I'm so happy and grateful to see her that I almost cry.

"Simon left," she tells me unnecessarily. "I decided to wait for you."

I barely take the time to thank her before I'm rushing her off to the parking lot.

"Simon sure drove off in a hurry," Beverly tells me as we drive to Sabrina's house. She gives me a curious glance. "He didn't say a word to anybody. He looked really, really angry, too."

It's obvious that she's just dying to know what's going on, but I'm in no mood to enlighten her. I just stare out the window and wish she would *hurry up*. Honestly, a slug could keep pace with Beverly. Simon will probably have left by the time we get there — if he decides to show up at all.

As soon as we get to Sabrina's, I jump out of the car and start searching for Simon.

I find him hiding out in the kitchen, pounding away at a bag of ice and putting the broken pieces into an ice bucket. Pete and Max are with him, kidding around with each other the way boys do. Then they see me and all conversation stops.

"Uh — Marie!" exclaims Pete. "Bev with you?"

I nod. "She's in the den."

161

"I'll help you look for her," says Max, and then they both skulk out like I've got the plague or something.

Simon keeps pounding at the ice as if his life depends upon it.

I clear my throat to get his attention, but he doesn't look up. "You shouldn't make snap assumptions, you know," I tell him.

He drops the bag of ice. "Don't play games with my head," he says. "I *saw* you with Brian."

"So?"

He shrugs. "So, I can put two and two together."

"Yeah, and get five! What you *saw* was on Brian's part, not mine."

"What I *saw* was you *kissing* him."

"That was a good-bye kiss, nothing more."

"Sure it was." Simon goes back to annihilating the ice.

"It was! I came out of the bathroom, Brian was there, waiting for me — would you stop with the ice, please? You're giving me a headache!"

"So what did the jock want? To tell you how much he enjoyed the play?"

"No," I say evenly. "As a matter of fact, he wanted to get back together with me."

"And what did you tell him?"

"What do you *think* I told him?"

"I don't know what to think!" he says. "I thought we had something going, and then I see you kissing your old boyfriend. You say the guy is after you again, and I ask myself why. Why would he be after you, when you told me he knew it was over for good. That was a lie, wasn't it?"

"No!"

Simon makes this sound of disbelief, like air hissing through his teeth.

"Well, it wasn't all a lie," I say. "How was I to know he — " I stop. Simon is now making vicious stabs at the ice with a sharp knife. And the look on his face!

"Well," I finish defensively, "I only lied to protect your feelings!"

"Do me a favor," he snarls, suddenly facing me. "Don't protect me. Just be straight with me for once."

"For once?"

"Yeah, that's right, for once in your life just finish with all the sugar-and-spice crap and give it to me straight. I can take it. Is it over with you and Brian or not?"

"Yes!"

This time he makes that hissing noise *and* he quirks up the eyebrow. The double whammy!

"Okay, I guess he thought he might have a chance to get back to the way things were," I admit. "Maybe I wasn't firm enough with him before. I just didn't want to make trouble! I don't like to hurt people's feelings."

"Yeah, I know, you're just *so* nice," he says sarcastically, rolling his eyes.

"Well, I wasn't so nice this time, all right? I had to tell him flat out that I wasn't interested, and it *hurt* him. Satisfied? Now he's angry at me, and you're angry at me, too!"

"He'll get over it," says Simon gruffly.

"Will you?"

"Aw, Marie — "

That's it. The fight's over. He's relented. But suddenly I decide that I'm not going to let him off that easily.

"This is the biggest night of my entire life," I tell him, stepping back and looking him straight in the eye, "and you almost totally ruined it!"

"Me?" he squeaks.

"Yeah, you. You should have stuck around back there. Then you could have seen for yourself that nothing was going on between me and Brian. Instead you assume the worst and go running off like some spoiled little kid!"

Simon puts his hands on his hips and glares at me, so much like a spoiled little kid that I almost laugh.

"And I used to think you were so mature!" I say. "So smart! So bursting with self-confidence! Ha! Boy, was I wrong!"

"Cut it out, Marie," he warns, moving threateningly towards me.

"Or you'll do what?"

"Or I'll — "

Then he kisses me, of course. Just like I knew he would. And it's such a great kiss, so warm and tingly, that I decided not to give him too hard a time about not trusting me and all that. I mean, it's very difficult to give someone a hard time when you're melting into his arms.

"You," he mutters in my ear, "are going to drive me up the wall."

"Don't dish it out if you can't take it," I reply as lightly as I can. Simon groans.

"No more arguing, okay?" He pushes my hair away

from my face and looks down at me with those honey-colored eyes. "Truce?"

"For now," I agree. "But you know, maybe arguing's not so bad, after all."

"*What?*" he exclaims, pulling back. "Okay, I give. Now I *know* I've cracked up if I'm starting to hear things that wild. You win. Get the straight jacket ready, and lock me up in the rubber room."

"I'll visit you every Sunday," I promise, and then I pull his head down for another kiss. A really long, intense, passionate kiss, the kind you see on *Santa Barbara* or read about in romance novels. Only this kiss is much, much better, because it's *real*. Also, Simon is one *fantastic* kisser.

I feel his arms tighten around me, which is a good thing, because my knees are feeling so wobbly that I'd fall down if he weren't holding me up. No exaggeration, this is the kind of kiss that not only curls your toes, but also curls your entire leg. Maybe your *entire* body.

Eventually we have to stop kissing and take the ice — before it melts, too — into the den. Music is playing loud, kids are dancing, and everybody is having a good time.

"Okay, partner," Simon says, taking my hand. "Let's join the party."

Other books you will enjoy,
about real kids like you!

point ® THRILLERS

Read them and *scream!*